The *Sister* SOLUTION

ALSO BY TRUDI TRUEIT

Secrets of a Lab Rat series

Stealing Popular

The Sister SOLUTION

BY TRUDI TRUEIT

ALADDIN M!X

NEW YORK   LONDON   TORONTO   SYDNEY   NEW DELHI

This book is a work of fiction. Any references to historical events, real people, or real places are used fictitiously. Other names, characters, places, and events are products of the author's imagination, and any resemblance to actual events or places or persons, living or dead, is entirely coincidental.

ALADDIN M!X

Simon & Schuster Children's Publishing Division

1230 Avenue of the Americas, New York, New York 10020

First Aladdin M!X edition September 2015

Text copyright © 2015 by Trudi Trueit

Cover illustration copyright © 2015 by Adrian Valencia

Also available in an Aladdin hardcover edition.

All rights reserved, including the right of reproduction in whole or in part in any form.

ALADDIN is a trademark of Simon & Schuster, Inc., and related logo is a registered trademark of Simon & Schuster, Inc.

ALADDIN M!X and related logo are registered trademarks of Simon & Schuster, Inc.

For information about special discounts for bulk purchases, please contact Simon & Schuster Special Sales at 1-866-506-1949 or business@simonandschuster.com.

The Simon & Schuster Speakers Bureau can bring authors to your live event. For more information or to book an event contact the Simon & Schuster Speakers Bureau at 1-866-248-3049 or visit our website at www.simonspeakers.com.

Book designed by Laura Lyn DiSiena

The text of this book was set in Palatino.

Manufactured in the United States of America 0815 OFF

10 9 8 7 6 5 4 3 2 1

Library of Congress Control Number 2014953869

ISBN 978-1-4814-3240-5 (hc)

ISBN 971-1-4814-3239-9 (pbk)

ISBN 978-1-4814-3241-2 (eBook)

✳ Contents ✳

For my sister, Lori Dru, and sisters everywhere

And for Sammy, a beacon of hope for many
and an inspiration to us all

*No one can annoy, embarrass,
scold, provoke, exasperate, wound,
or love you like your sister*

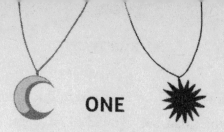

ONE

The Ninth Ring of Saturn

"I SEE SATURN!" EDEN SQUINTS, AND HER CINNAMON-brown eyes disappear beneath lashes plumped to the max with glittery mascara. "I think."

A second from biting into my taco, I freeze.

And wait.

And wait.

A chunk of salsa plops onto my plate. I can't stand it any longer. "Well?"

"Yep. It's her. Saturn is buying a salad with app— no, pear slices."

A wave of fear—a tsunami of terror, actually— surges through me. Saturn is our code for Patrice

Houston, the most popular girl in the eighth grade. If she's at the salad bar, it means I have less than thirty seconds to tame my lion's mane of red hair, shrink four inches, get my ears pierced, buy some new clothes, and make over my entire personality.

Twenty-nine . . . twenty-eight . . .

Eden and I gave Patrice the name Saturn because she has rings of friends circling her. The closer friend you are, the closer you get to sit to her at lunch. Eden Tran and I are in one of the outer rings. Okay, the ninth and last ring. Sometimes, she'll talk to us on her way to her table if *we* don't have food in our mouths or are wearing something cute and if *she* hasn't broken a nail, failed a test, or had a fight with the boy she likes. I know that's a lot of "ifs," but when you've been working your way toward the inner orbit for seven months the way Eden and I have, you take whatever you can get.

Once, when Eden was absent a few months ago, Patrice invited me to sit with her group at lunch. It was my first time in the first ring. I ended up *right beside* Saturn. We were so close Patrice nearly knocked over my apple juice. It was beyond epic. However,

I hadn't been there more than a few minutes when I knew something was wrong. Patrice's pretty face was all caved in. I watched her stab about a hundred holes into her baked chicken before, finally, getting up the nerve to ask, "Is everything okay?"

"I'm in a colossally bad mood," she hissed.

"Anything I can do?"

"I doubt it. I have a dumb photography assignment due in Hargrove's class. We're supposed to do a study of humanity, whatever that means."

I couldn't believe it! Not only did I love photography, but I'd had Hargrove for art last semester. I knew what the assignment was, and what he was looking for, and what he was looking for were pictures with emotion. Was it possible that I, the ordinarily average Samantha Eleanor Tremayne, could help the supremely popular Patrice Houston? I whipped out my cell phone. I explained the assignment and started showing her pictures I'd taken so she'd understand what to do. Her face brightened. Scrolling through some of my best shots, Patrice said the nicest thing anybody has ever said to me. She said, "You're a great photographer, Sammi." I wish she would have said it loud enough for the whole first ring to hear, but you can't have everything. Patrice even let me snap a selfie of the two of us before lunch ended. I'll never forget that as long as I live. Neither will Eden. She was bummed she'd missed the entire thing.

"Tanith is with her but I don't see Cara anywhere," Eden says as if she is broadcasting a golf tournament on TV. "Mercy is missing too. Maybe she came in the south entrance and is already in line." Dark eyes scan the cafeteria. "No sign of SGB either." SGB (super gorgeous boy) is our code for Noah Whitehall, Patrice's on-again, off-again crush. Current status: off-again.

Twenty . . . Nineteen . . .

I chew on my lower lip. "Do you think they're finished for good?"

"Amy said Desiree heard from Cara that Tanith said she was pretty sure they were, but that was first period and it's been a whole three hours since then so who knows?" Eden flicks her long, silky, black hair over her shoulders. If I tried that move, my garnet-red tumbleweed hair would bounce forward and smother me to death. Hallelujah for gargantuan barrettes like the big gold clip that's holding my giant mass of hair back right now.

Eden strikes a pose. "Sammi, how do I look? Be honest."

I don't have to lie. "Stunning, as always."

"The planet approaches." Eden glues on a smile. "Look happy."

Ten . . . nine . . .

I take a deep breath, and the smell of refried beans and onions burns my nostrils. I hold my taco casually in my left hand to make it look as if I am in no hurry to eat because my best friend and I are having the most fascinating conversation in the history of Tonasket Middle School.

"Get ready," directs Eden between clenched teeth, "in five . . . four . . . three . . ."

We always finish the countdown silently so Saturn doesn't hear.

Two . . . one . . .

"Ah-ha-ha-ha-ha-ha." I let out a chuckle and toss my head.

Ka-zing!

I feel a thump on the back of my skull. I turn my

head in time to see my gold Celtic-knot barrette catapult across the cafeteria. Shoot! I don't know how far the metal missile streaks or where it lands because soon after, I am blinded by a woolen blanket of my own hair.

Crunch!

Melted cheese is sliding over my fingers. This cannot be happening! Is that laughter? It is. And it is not coming from Eden. Using my unslimed hand, I do my best to push the hair from my eyes. Beside me stands a pair of slim legs wearing black tights with a cute flower pattern. I tip my head, eyes traveling upward over a short black skirt and black turtleneck with red trim. A red headband arcs over smooth, shiny wheat-colored hair. It perfectly matches the turtleneck trim and ten long fingernails. Five of those fingers hold a tray with a salad, while the other five tap her hip. Patrice Houston, however, isn't interested in me. She is gazing at something or someone across the room— probably Noah. Tanith West is beside Patrice and she *is* looking down at me. Tanith's mocha ponytail curls over one shoulder. Her shirt is tucked halfway into a new pair of three-hundred-dollar Bitterroot jeans I would give a kidney to have in my own closet.

Holding her tray against her, Tanith coolly raises an eyebrow. "Defective taco, Sammi?"

I turn my wrist over, striking a pose. "It's only a small—"

Crack! The taco shell collapses. An avalanche of beef, cheese, lettuce, and salsa spills over my hand and onto the tray. Eden's eyes vanish into her forehead. I am blowing it for us big time. I start grabbing napkins.

"Bummer," says Tanith in an unsympathetic tone.

"That's why *we* never eat tacos," says Patrice with a giggle. "So you guys want to sit with us?"

I gulp so loud everyone hears it. "Us? You? Now?"

"Yes. You. Us. Now." Tanith snorts. "Cara is on a field trip and Mercy has some kind of wicked cold germ."

"We'll be right there," Eden says, before I can sputter more nonsense.

"You know where to find us," says Patrice. "Tanith, what are you waiting for? Go."

"Forgive *meee*," Tanith snaps, and leads the way down the aisle.

We wait until Patrice and Tanith are out of earshot

to do our victory cry. We hook pinkies and quietly say, "Skuh-wee!" Neither of us can remember why we started celebrating this way, but we have been doing it since the fifth grade. It's pretty childish, I know, but it's tradition and tradition tops maturity any day.

"Sammi, when we get over there you've got to keep it together," says Eden, wrapping up her baked potato. "You can't be breaking taco shells or getting lettuce stuck in your teeth. If we have another food catastrophe, we'll get banished to the outer edge of the universe."

We pause from packing to glance at Lauren Berring and Hanna Welch, eating together under the growling tiger mascot painted on the wall. Last fall the two of them were in Saturn's first ring, meaning they sat at her table. By Christmas they were four tables away. Now, three months later, they float alone in the vast outer reaches of middle school space. Nobody knows what happened. Those of us trying to orbit closer to Saturn are too afraid to ask—too afraid that if we know, we might end up like Lauren and Hanna.

As we head toward Saturn, Eden hisses, "Do not do that thing with your face."

"What thing?"

"That thing you do when something's bothering you."

"What *are* you talking about?"

"This." She scrunches her nose up. Eden looks as if she has caught a whiff of the boys locker room after a track meet.

"I don't do that."

"You do so."

And we are here, so I can't insist that my BFF is TCD (totally and completely delusional). At the moment we have a bigger problem than my face. There are no empty places at Patrice and Tanith's table. The spots left by Cara and Mercy have been taken by India Martello and Desiree Pierce, who are much higher in the order of orbit than we are. I look at Eden. What are we supposed to do now? Tanith sees us and points a couple of tables over, where there are two open seats. It's a ring farther out than we expected, but there's not much we can do about it. We obey, setting our lunches next to Stella Nguyen and Bridget Forrester.

"Hi," we say.

"Hi," they say.

I'm nervous. It's been awhile since we last ate with Stella and Bridget. I don't know them very well. I want to start a conversation, but I can't think of anything cute or funny to say. My little sister, Jorgianna, always has some kind of crazy piece of trivia on the tip of her tongue. She is a genius. No kidding. Jorgianna is eleven, but tests at an eleventh-grade level. Everyone knows my sister will do something remarkable with her life. I, on the other hand, am not expected to do much with mine. I have a solid B average, am fourth-chair clarinet, and have never won anything. Not a photography contest. Not a spelling bee. Not even a dumb jar of honey at the county fair.

I am sculpting my applesauce into a four-leaf clover when Eden catches my eye. She shakes her head. I must be making The Face. I try to relax my jaw, but I can't see myself. I have a feeling I look like I've got a bad sunburn.

"I love your sweater," Bridget says to me. "Moss is my favorite color."

"Mine too. My sister made it for my birthday."

"She made that?"

"Jorgianna is super crafty. She taught herself from a book she got at the library. Tried to teach me, too, but I never got the hang of it."

"Me neither," says Stella. "My aunt got me started, but forgot to show me how to finish off. I have a scarf that's ten feet long—so far."

We laugh, and pretty soon the four of us are talking about all kinds of things, like the new blue-raspberry gum in the vending machine that always steals your money, and Principal Ostrum's love of hand sanitizer.

The bell rings.

"See you guys tomorrow?" asks Stella.

Eden and I nod. We aren't sure Patrice will approve the idea, but we hope so. Boy, do we hope so.

"You know what this means," says Eden, once we dump our trash.

Of course I do! We are now in Saturn's fourth ring. Maybe this time it will stick.

We grab pinkies again. "Skuh-wee!"

There is a tap on my shoulder. Thinking it's Bridget or Stella, I spin quickly on my heel. Too quickly. I topple forward, crushing the toes of—oh no!—my secret crush, a.k.a. SGB, a.k.a. Noah Whitehall. "Sorry." I regain my balance. "You okay?"

"No damage," says Noah. "You?"

"Fine." I sound like a squeaky violin.

I look into Noah's eyes. I have grown four inches in the past eight months and am now taller than two-thirds of the boys in the eighth grade. But today, here and now, Noah and I are eye to eye. And his eyes, I must remember to tell Eden, are nice. Really, really nice. Unusual. The lightest of greens with gold flecks and not a trace of the sarcasm you typically see in a boy's eyes. A million thoughts storm my brain. I never noticed that little dimple in the middle of his chin and he smells like whipped cream and he sure does look good in that heather gray long-sleeve tee with the sleeves pushed up. I feel dizzy. It could be because we are standing next to the soup and it's French onion soup day (heavy on the onions). Or it could be him.

Noah opens his hand to reveal my gold Celtic-knot barrette. "Yours?"

"Yuh-huh."

Shoot! Did I just say "yuh-huh" to the cutest boy in the universe?

"Thanks." I take the clip. My fingers brush his hand, and all the blood in my body rushes up to play connect the dots with the freckles on my cheeks and nose. I can feel tiny beads of sweat on my forehead.

Why am I getting all flustered? Boys never notice me, especially with Eden around. We are both thirteen, but she looks fifteen. Eden is slim, yet athletic, with toned olive arms and legs in perfect proportion to the rest of her body. My body, on the other hand, is in rebellion. It likes to surprise me with random growth spurts. One day my arms are too long for my sleeves and the next my feet are bursting out of my boots— my practically new Daisy Chain hunter-green ankle boots I'd wanted forever and had been so careful not to scuff, scratch, or get even one itty bitty smudge on. I ended up giving them to my little sister, Jorgianna, whose fashion style can best be described as Triple G (ghastly, gaudy, and gross). My sister has a huge vocabulary, but the word subtle is not in it. Jorgianna paired my heavenly boots with a gold-fringed top, a red-and-white gingham overhaul-style jumper, and neon-yellow tights. She looked like a picnic basket exploded on her.

Noah sweeps aside long, dark bangs. "That thing is pretty aerodynamic."

"Please don't tell me it hit you."

"Okay, I won't, but . . ." He rubs his shoulder.

"I am so, so sorry."

Could this day get any worse?

"Seriously," Noah rushes to say, "I barely felt it. Well . . . see ya, Sammi." He said my name! My secret crush, a.k.a. SGB, a.k.a. Noah Whitehall actually said my name! For several seconds I hear our flute section playing my favorite section of the Mozart Flute Concerto No. 1, but without Tanith, who is always out of tune and one beat behind everyone else.

"See ya . . ." I let the sentence hang in the air. If I say Noah's name, I'm afraid he'll know by the tone of my voice that I like him. So I don't. I can't. What if he doesn't like me back? Of course he doesn't like me back. He likes Patrice. I scan the cafeteria for Saturn. There she is! Tanith is orbiting her. They are heading toward the exit at the opposite end of the long room, yet looking—more like glaring—in our direction.

"Be careful, you don't want Patrice to see you flirting with SGB," says Eden.

"I wasn't flirting."

"Of course you weren't. And he was definitely not flirting back." My best friend gives me a sideways smile.

I roll my eyes, but can't help returning the grin. SGB flirting with me? That's a laugh and a half. He barely knows I exist. Well, that's not completely true. He knows my name. Plus, of all the kids in the cafeteria, my barrette hit Noah. That has to mean something. As my sister would say, it's serendipity.

It was meant to be.

TWO

Sunbeam

I LOVE IT. I HAVE NO IDEA WHAT THE SCULPTURE IS, but maybe that's *why* I love it. It could be a coiled neon-green papier-mâché snake. Or an extraterrestrial with no sensory organs. Or maybe it's an ordinary garden hose with an attitude. Whatever it is, it's covered in a layer of uncooked spinach pasta shells.

My stomach lets out a growl. I guess I should have had dinner with Sammi, Mom, and Dad, but spicy chilidogs are not something you should eat when you are nervous. And I am beyond nervous. I am petrified. My sculpture is on display here too. It's in the next gallery.

My father tips his head. "You've found an interesting one, Sunbeam." Dad always calls me Sunbeam. My sister, Sammi, is Moonbeam. I have no complaints. I'd rather be a blazing star that's twenty seven million degrees Fahrenheit than a cold hunk of rock any day. Okay, in all fairness the moon does get to more than two hundred degrees Fahrenheit during the day, but then can drop down to negative two hundred degrees at night. That's because the moon has no atmosphere to hold in the heat or cold. I like to think I have plenty of atmosphere.

"What is it, Jorgianna?" asks my mother, her head bending to match mine.

People think because my intelligence is well above average for someone who is eleven years, six months, and twenty-three days old, I have all the answers. I don't, of course—only about 96.3 percent of them. "It's art, Mom."

The lines in her forehead deepen. "Are those wires sticking out the top supposed to be antennae or hooks?"

"Yes," I say.

I walk on. I don't have to look back to know she is still frowning, but soon she'll figure out there is nothing to figure out. Or maybe not. Being a scientist in the food industry, my mom deals in facts. Everything must have a reason for being, and that reason must be clearly stated on the label. My dad writes instructional manuals for medical equipment, but he's also an artist (acrylics, mostly). I know he'll be able to throw out a few suggestions to make her feel better.

I pause inside the entrance of the next gallery. It's a large A-frame room with a shiny bamboo floor and arctic-white walls. Track lights hang from the crossbeams, spotlighting the various drawings, paintings, photographs, and sculptures on display. The smell of fresh buttered popcorn from the lobby drifts in to almost, but not quite, disguise the odor of paint. Parents and kids mill about, studying the artwork done by Tonasket elementary and middle school students.

The ends of my fingertips are tingling. I know where my sculpture is. It's in the far corner. I'm not yet ready to find out what the judges thought about it, though. I decide to take my time getting there. I start at the outside wall closest to the door. I study a ceramic sunflower with a broken stem, a vase with flowers on it, and a muted watercolor painting of—oh, please! Not another sunflower. This makes five sunflowers for the night, so far. I stop to look at a sickly unicorn with a pink head, blue body, and a purple tail. Its satellite dish–size head is weighing down four chopstick-thin legs. It's a miracle the poor animal hasn't collapsed.

An older girl is staring too—at me. Grayish-blue eyes widen as she takes in my short, choppy, so-blond-it's-almost-white hair. I put a lot of spikes in it, especially for tonight. Sammi said all I needed was a big chain around my neck and I'd look like one of those medieval mace balls. I had planned to dye the tips silver, too, but my sister had a fit. Sammi snatched the dye box right out of my hand. "No."

"It's light silver."

"No."

"You'll hardly be able to see it."

"No."

"Why not? You're babysitting Paisley. You won't even be there."

"Plenty of people I know *are* going to be there. I'll

never hear the end of it if you show up looking like the tin man. Jorgianna, I don't want you making an idiot of yourself."

"Hardly. My IQ is—"

"A bazillion and two, I know. You might have a high IQ, but your taste score is, like, four."

"It is not! You're the one with no sense of fashion. All you ever wear is brown or black. Talk about boring—"

"Temper, Jorgianna."

I growled. Why is it every time somebody tells you to calm down it only makes you madder?

"I love how you manage to somehow squeeze your IQ score into every conversation," said my sister.

"It's not *every* conversation," I shouted as she left the bathroom with *my* box of dye. "Sammi, give me back—"

"Not a chance."

"You care too much about what other people think."

"And you don't care enough."

She is wrong about that. I do care. I only pretend

not to. I've never had a best friend, unless you count Darwin, but he's a guinea pig. It would be nice to have a friend that's my own species.

I gave in to my sister on the hair, but not my outfit—*never* my outfit. I might do all my homework and ace almost every test to please everybody else, but fashion is for me. I love the freedom it gives me to express myself. Tonight I've got on a parrot-green sweater. Dyed-to-match pom-poms trim the crew-neck and dangle from the short, puffed sleeves. Below that, I'm wearing a fuchsia poof skirt with white polka dots, white lace tights, and white vinyl Victorian ankle boots. Bright green and pink for a bright girl in a bright mood—that's me!

I turn to inspect the girl who is inspecting me. She has on a butter-colored tee with a draped neck and the most expensive Bitterroot designer jeans you can buy (the ocean-blue swirl on the front pocket gives it away). Parted by a thin yellow hairband, light-blond hair falls to her elbows. She is wearing a pair of four-hundred-dollar Sassy Girl sandals, and her toes are painted clear with a touch of glitter. A tiny gold shamrock hangs around her neck, with matching shamrocks hanging from her ears.

"I don't mean to be rude," she says, "it's just . . . I mean, I was wondering—"

I roll my eyes. "Yes, I know Halloween is seven months away, and no, I am not joining the circus, and yes, my mother knows I left the house looking like this. Did I cover everything?"

"I . . . uh . . . guess so."

I lean in to take a closer look at the skinny unicorn. I can feel myself start to relax. I didn't mean to hurt her feelings, but the third degree gets old. Also, my sister is right. I do have a bit of a temper. Okay, more than a bit.

"I don't blame you for being defensive," says Shamrock. "All I meant . . . I mean, what I was going to say was I think your outfit is amazing to the tenth power."

I eye her suspiciously. Technically, there is no such math equation.

"Your hair, too. The spikes are edgy but not over the top."

I exhale. "Thanks."

"Your style is so fun." Shamrock stands back to

study me as if I am one of the art exhibits. "It's cool, yet with a touch of Alice in Wonderland. Very quirky but also—what's the word I'm looking for?" She snaps her fingers. "Chic."

Did I hear angels? Someone in this town, finally, gets me.

"Thanks," I say again, this time with real feeling.

"I really like the way you've put all those colors together," she says. "That's where I have trouble. I never know what goes with what."

"You can't go wrong with complementary colors," I say. "Those are the ones that are opposite each other on the color wheel."

"Color wheel? I think we have one hanging up in my art class at school, but I can't remember which colors are opposite each other."

"Yellow and purple. Peach and navy."

She motions to my outfit. "Pink and green?"

"Right." I grin. "My dad's an artist. He says complementary colors bring out the best in each other."

"I'll remember that." She gasps. "Is that an X.O. Minxx sweater?"

"You know your clothes! It took me six months to

save for it." It is one of the few designer pieces I own that didn't come from the Helping Hands thrift store. I have a scout on the inside scoring me some cute clothes at great prices, otherwise known as my grandmother. She volunteers there every Wednesday and Friday.

"The pom-poms are adorbs."

"Thanks." I move my arm, making the pom-poms on the sleeve wiggle. "My sister says I look like a human sombrero."

"Your sister is wrong."

I like this girl.

"Sorry if I seemed a bit hostile earlier," I say.

"Huh?"

"Mad."

"No big dealy woo." Shamrock glances at the creepy unicorn between us. "So what do you think?"

"All that's missing is a rainbow," I say. Dang! What was I thinking? What if the hideous pink sculpture is hers? I scramble to add, "But the . . . uh . . . head is . . . unique."

"For sure. I'll bet that thing bites the dust in an hour."

Whew! It's not hers.

"Check it out." She points to the red ribbon tacked to the side of the display case. "My Little Mutant Unicorn here got third place. Leave it to Mrs. Vanderslice and the judges to reward cliché."

"Mrs. Vanderslice is judging?"

"Uh-huh."

I'm doomed. Mrs. Vanderslice is our school superintendent. She usually wears polyester pantsuits in the same color scheme as the M&M'S they sell around Easter time. She's under five feet tall, but her beehive bun adds about a foot to her height. It leans at about a seventy-degree angle, but can tip farther if wind speeds hit more than ten miles per hour. Mrs. Vanderslice is looking for art that matches her style. Old-fashioned. Sweet. Pastel. What was I thinking? I should have done a butterfly sculpture. Or a charcoal self-portrait. Or a sunflower *anything*.

"Come on." Shamrock latches on to my arm. "There *is* one piece in this place that gives me hope for our generation."

She leads me across the floor. I hesitate when I see we are headed to the far corner of the room, but her grip is firm. We stop at the side of a display stand holding a wooden cube about two-feet tall by two-feet wide. The geography of Washington State is painted in oils in one continuous landscape around the four vertical sides. A few three-dimensional landmarks carved in wood have been attached: the Cascade Mountains, the Space Needle, and a little schoolhouse in Tonasket. On the back side a flat, wooden, doglike tail is attached to the cube with a hinge. The upturned tail has been painted a deep sapphire blue to match the water. The top of the box is open.

An elbow nudges me. "You have to get really close to see all of the detail. See, there's Mount Rainier. And Seattle. There's even a little 3-D Space Needle. Look, over here is Tonasket. It must have taken forever to paint."

"I'm sure it didn't—"

"Oh, wait. You have to see the best part." Shamrock hauls me around to the back of the display where a small set of stairs has been pushed up against the stand.

"Go on up. Look inside."

"It's all right—"

"You *must* look."

"Okay, okay." Hurrying up the three white steps, I peek inside the cube. It's painted black and filled with trash—syringes, latex gloves, pop cans, plastic bags, lightbulbs, batteries, hot dog packages, junk mail—all resting on a bed of sand and broken seashells.

Shamrock is waiting for me at the bottom of the steps. Her hands are clasped. Her eyes are wide. "You get it, don't you? See, we are slowly ruining our planet with dangerous chemicals, toxic junk, and wasteful packaging. We bury it under the surface and try to pretend nothing is wrong, but it's still there, destroying us from the inside out. But it's not all doom and gloom. As long as we are alive, there's still hope we can turn things around. That's what the dog's tail means." She moves the tail back and forth on its hinge. "At least, I think it's a dog's tail. What do you think?"

"I think—"

"It looks like a Labrador's tail to me and they are always happy dogs, right?"

"Maybe not *always*, but—"

"I like that about it, don't you? I like it when environmental art is . . . oh, you know . . . what's the word I'm looking for?"

"Optimistic?"

"Yes!"

"Let's hope the judges do too," I mutter.

"I'm sure they do. It won its category, so it's in the running for Best in Show."

"It is?" I hurry around to the only side of the stand I haven't yet seen. A blue first-place ribbon hangs next to the artist identification card. My heart is pounding so loudly I can barely hear Shamrock, who is still jabbering away. ". . . and see how the water glistens? It's like you can almost see the waves hitting the shore. I wonder how the artist got it to sparkle like that."

"Pearlized powder added to the base paint."

Gray-blue eyes look at me, then the cube, then me again. "How do you know?"

"It's . . . sort of . . . I mean . . . It's my piece."

She slaps her cheeks, making her clover earrings swing. "Oh man. Are you kidding? I dragged you over here to look at your own sculpture!"

"It's all right."

"How dumb could I possibly be?"

"Really, it's okay." I should have confessed sooner, but I didn't want to frighten her. That's what I do. I scare kids. When you're smart, kids assume you want to use your intelligence to make everyone else in the class look bad. But you don't. You can't help having a high IQ. It happens to you, like having a second toe longer than the first or being allergic to strawberries.

I need to change the subject, to get it off me. "Do you have a piece in the show too?"

"Yeah." She crosses an eye in. "It's not nearly as good as yours."

"A sculpture?"

"A photograph. It's in the last—"

"Jorgianna!" Mrs. Vanderslice's voice fills every inch of space between the floor and the rafters. The superintendent is heading toward me. She is in a spearmint-green suit and matching pumps. Her tall spun-cotton-candy beehive is only a few degrees off its vertical axis. Four adults are in formation a few steps behind her; two on the right and two on the left. Everyone is carrying clipboards and looking stern. Did I get disqualified?

"Y . . . yes?" I gulp.

Mrs. Vanderslice throws open her arms and, suddenly, I am engulfed in the eye of a mint-green tornado. She starts to squeeze. Gasping for air inside her marshmallow clinch, I hear a muffled "Well done, my dear. Well done." A second before one of my lungs ruptures, the superintendent releases me. Someone calls, "Smile," so I do and several camera flashes go off, creating a haze of fireworks. With patriotic dots still floating in front of me, I catch a glimpse of a ribbon the color of ripe eggplant. The words BEST IN SHOW are stamped in gold letters in the center of the rosette. This is . . . for me?

I turn to Mrs. Vanderslice. "You liked it?"

The Leaning Tower of Vanderslice sways. "Very much."

"I was worried. I thought you wouldn't—"

"Uh, uh, uh." She wags a finger. "An artist must never let fear of judgment keep her from expressing what must be expressed. If people get it, bravo! If they don't, it is their loss. Remember, Jorgianna, 'to thine own self be true,' as the great Winston Churchill said."

"Um . . . I think that was Shakespeare."

Mrs. Vanderslice is not listening. She has side-stepped me to greet my parents and engulf them in her green vortex.

Then it's true. I won. *I really won!*

I wish Sammi were here, but I suppose it's for the best that she isn't. It wouldn't be good for us. We aren't as close as we should be. It's my fault. I win too much and she wins too little. I know it's a problem, but I don't know how to fix it. I don't know how to be anyone other than who I am.

My sister thinks she doesn't measure up to me, but she's wrong. I make people uncomfortable. Sammi puts them at ease. She can get even the shyest person in the room to talk. She's beautiful, too. My sister is tall and graceful, with thick flame-red hair and eyes the color of London-blue topaz. Freckles dust her nose and cheeks and neck, as if someone has blown gold glitter into her face and some of it fell onto her shoulders. People may be impressed by me, but they are charmed by Sammi.

"Such a dynamic piece." Mrs. Vanderslice's voice

rises for the benefit of the growing crowd. The four people behind her nod enthusiastically. "We are enormously proud to have Jorgianna Tremayne's piece *My Corner of the World* move on to represent the Tonasket School District at the state level in the student art competition."

Everyone applauds.

A woman rushes toward me. "Congratulations, Jorgianna!"

"Banana!" I hug her. My grandmother was not named after a fruit. Her actual name is Brooke-Ann, but when my sister was little she had trouble saying Nanna Brook-Ann. It came out Banana, and that is what our family has called her ever since. "I'm so glad you made it," I say.

"Are you kidding?" She shakes her key ring. "The shop is closed up tight. I wouldn't miss my granddaughter's artistic debut for anything."

I step aside. "So what do you think?"

Putting a hand on her heart, she gasps. "Oh, Jorgianna. I think *it* is extraordinary and I think *you* are a great blue heron soaring among mallards."

Banana gets another hug for that. Someone is tugging on one of my sleeve pom-poms. I twirl to tell the child to stop, but it's not a kid. It's Shamrock!

"Nice job, Quirky Chic."

"Thanks." I cannot hide my happiness. The formula is usually: Jorgianna wins = kids scatter. Shamrock has discovered a new equation and I am thrilled!

"My dad's picking me up in a few," she says. "I just wanted to say it was a blast to meet you."

"Same here."

"Bye."

I watch her go. She takes quick, small steps on her tiptoes like a ballet dancer.

"Wait," I call. "What about *your* photo? I want to see it—"

"Last room," she calls back.

"But which one is it? You never told me your name."

She keeps going. She isn't going to tell me who she is! I *did* frighten her away. Halfway across the floor, Shamrock twirls. Her hair flutters out like a golden cape. She flings both arms wide. "Patrice. My name is Patrice Houston."

THREE

The Six-Percent Sister

I TIP MY HEAD SO MY CHIN IS RESTING ON SAMMI'S doorframe.

It's impossible for her *not* to see me. I am wearing an oversized orange tee with bright pink diagonal stripes, a pair of turquoise leggings, and fuzzy hunter-green socks. In jeans and a faded brown tee, my sister sits cross-legged in the middle of her white comforter. She has a yellow legal pad balanced on one knee. Sunshine streams through the window, setting the burnt-orange and sienna tones in her thick curls on fire.

I can't wait forever. "Sam?"

"Read the sign, Jorgianna," she says, not looking up.

"Your door was open."

"Read the sign."

My sister likes to whine that I am, "always bugging her," which is not true. First, "always" is an absolute, so you should not say "always" unless there isn't even a sliver of a chance you could be wrong (same goes for "never"). Second, I have proof. I did a few calculations and found Sammi spends approximately 94 percent of her time doing things that don't—repeat, *do not*—involve me, like sleeping, showering, going to school, studying, etc. Turns out I am a participant in only about 6 percent of her life. 6 percent! That's a long, long way from "always." Certain she would be impressed, I showed her my math. She wasn't. Instead, my sister took it as a challenge to decrease the amount of time she spent with me. Sammi bought a big piece of white poster board at the craft store, cut out a huge circle, divided the circle into eight equal parts, and colored each slice. She wrote different things in each slice, such as *Sammi is Sleeping*, *Sammi is Eating*, or *Sammi is Practicing Her Clarinet*. She swiped the second hand from our mom's broken rooster clock and attached it in the middle of the circle with a brad. Now it hangs on her bedroom door so she can spin the second hand to whatever slice of the pie chart she wants me to see. My favorite is *Sammi Wants to be Alone*. Talk about a drama queen. Sammi's door looks like *Wheel of Fortune*. Currently the arrow on *Wheel of Paranoid Sister* is pointing to *Sammi is Studying*.

I stretch into her room. "It's important."

"Is the house on fire?"

"No."

"Then make like eggs and scramble, will you? I'm working on a story for language arts."

"Do you want me to—?"

"Jorgianna, do I have to close my door?"

"Okay, I'm leaving. I just thought you'd want to know *Mom* is making dinner."

Her head pops up. "Why didn't you say so?"

"I tried—"

"Where's Dad?"

"He's fixing Mrs. Merrill's fence."

Sammi flings the pad away. "What's she making?"

"I'm not sure. When I left, she was chopping pickles."

Two feet hit the floor. "Why does she keep trying to cook?"

"She got a promotion at work. Her confidence is up."

She flies down the stairs with me a half second behind her. We skid into the kitchen. I nearly hit the counter, but Sammi spins, grabs my waist, and keeps me from smashing into the granite.

Our mother glances up from murdering a sweet pickle. "Hi, girls."

"What'cha doing?" asks Sammi, gasping.

"Fixing dinner. Your dad is going to be late." She moves a wood bowl filled with peaches aside. Opening one of the bottom cabinets, she pulls out a rectangular clear glass casserole dish. "The Fiesta Tuna Surprise casserole recipe on the back of that can of soup sounded good. Jorgianna, can you get some radishes—"

"No!"

Sammi glares at me. "She means we promised Dad we'd make dinner tonight."

Our mother raises an eyebrow. She is on to us. "There isn't much in the fridge."

"We already worked out what we're making," Sammi says in her most soothing voice. "We'll call you when dinner's ready. Relax. Put your feet up. Read a book." Once Mom is safely out of the kitchen, my sister swings toward me. Her topaz eyes are huge. "So what are we making?"

I already have an idea. "Get milk and eggs. Butter, too."

While Sammi heads to the fridge, I go to the pantry for sugar, flour, and sea salt. I scan the shelves to see what else we have to work with. Green beans? No. Mushrooms? Ick. Sardines? Double ick. Maple syrup. Yes! A second before I close the door behind me, I see a bag of walnuts and grab them. I dump everything on the counter next to the ingredients my sister has brought. I slide the bowl of peaches over too. Holding a blue elastic hair band between her teeth, Sammi sweeps her hair back with both hands. "Well?"

"We're making crepes."

Lines squiggle their way across her forehead as she wraps the elastic band around her hair to make a high ponytail. "I've never made crepes."

"Me neither."

"Maybe we shouldn't—"

"I saw a chef make them on TV once."

"Okay, then." Sammi knows I am a quick study. Once is usually all it takes.

I tell Sammi to whip four eggs while I melt three tablespoons of butter in a frying pan on the stove. We pour the butter and eggs into the blender, and add a cup of flour, a quarter-teaspoon of sea salt, and one and a half cups of milk. I snap on the lid and give her the thumbs up. Sammi hits puree and waits for my signal. After about thirty seconds I see bubbles forming on top. I gesture for her to shut off the blender. "Now we let the batter sit for a bit. Do you want to slice peaches or chop walnuts?"

"I'll do the walnuts." She has taken the harder task.

Tap, tap, tap. Her knife hits the chopping block with careful strokes, even as she watches me out of the corner of her eye. "Be careful. Dad just had those sharpened."

"I will."

After a few more minutes. "Jorgianna?"

"Yes?"

"What exactly is a crepe?"

"A thin pancake, rolled or folded with filling inside."

"Oh! That sounds yummy."

"They're French. It's tradition to fill them with meat, cheese, fruit—"

"Or walnuts," she says, making a mountain from the nuts she's chopped.

I scoop the sliced peaches onto a small plate. Turning the stove to medium heat, I put a small pat of butter into the frying pan to melt. I pour some of the batter into the pan and swirl it around to coat the bottom. I let it cook for a couple of minutes, then slide the spatula under one side and carefully lift the delicate pancake. "It's ready to flip," I say, and slide the spatula all the way around the perimeter to loosen it. I try to turn the crepe, but one edge sticks and pulls the whole thing apart. "Oh, crap!"

Sammi snickers. "You mean 'oh, crepe.' It's okay. The first pancake always sticks." She pours more batter into the measuring cup. "Try it again. The second one will be better."

She is right. It is better. And the third better still.

We get a good routine going. Sammi measures the batter and hands it to me. I pour, then turn the crepe when it's ready. I signal it's done. She holds out the plate while I slide the spatula under each delicate, golden circle and place it on the growing stack. After six crepes, I offer her the spatula. "You want to make one?"

"Better not. I inherited Mom's cooking gene."

"If you mess it up, there's enough batter for more, but you won't. It's easy."

"For you, maybe," she murmurs, but then says, "I'll try."

"In France, February second is *La Chandeleur*," I say, stepping aside to let her pour batter into the pan. "National Crepe Day. I read all about it. They have crepe-flipping contests."

"Even *I* can flip a pancake."

"Without a spatula?"

"Oh!"

"One tradition is to flip with one hand, while holding a gold coin in the other hand. If you catch the crepe in the pan, it means you'll have good luck with money."

"And if you don't?"

"I guess you'll have crepe á la lint."

She laughs and slips the spatula under the edge of the pancake. "Ready to turn."

"Try it, Sam. No spat. Flick of the wrist. I dare you."

She gives me the evil eye as she slides the flat rubber utensil all the way around the edge of the pancake. Instead of turning the crepe, however, Sammi carefully sets the spatula down next to the burner. She picks up the pan. What's this? My always-follow-the-rules, never-take-a-challenge, mondo-barrette-wearing sister is going to flip this crepe with a flick of the wrist! I give her some tossing room. Sammi jiggles the pan back and forth. She glances up at the ceiling, then down at the pan. Deep in concentration, she sucks in her lower lip. Her wrist goes rigid. Sammi lowers her arm. As I watch her bring it up, I hold my breath. She's going to do it! She's going to . . .

"I can't!" she squeals, putting the pan back on the stove.

"Scaredy cat."

"You think it's so easy? Bet you can't do it."

"What do I get if I win?"

Sammi lifts a shoulder.

"It's a bet. I have to win something."

"You win enough as it is. What do I get if you miss?"

"What do you want?"

"You have to clean our bathroom for the next three months."

"Ew."

"That's what I want," says Sammi.

"If I win, you have to go to the Whitaker Gallery to see my artwork."

"I've seen it, remember?"

"Not in a real gallery. Not under the lights. Not on a nice display stand with steps. Not with the first-place ribbon and the Best in Show ribbon—"

"Okay, okay."

I want my sister to be proud of me, of course, but it's more than that. I want Sammi to feel like when I win, she wins, because that's how I think of it. She doesn't, though. Maybe this bet isn't a good idea. If I flip the crepe perfectly, which I probably will, it'll be one more in the win column for me and one more in the loss column for her. "Maybe we should finish up," I say. "Let's skip the bet—"

"No you don't. No backsies. But *all* of it has to land in the pan, Jorgianna."

"Piece of cake. I mean, piece of pancake."

She rolls her eyes. Cracking my neck and wiggling my arms, I get into crepe-flipping stance (knees apart and slightly bent). I'll bet there's an equation for the perfect flip. Let's see . . . the angular velocity of the pancake would be equal to the square root of pi times the gravity divided by the distance from my elbow to the center of the pancake times five, or maybe it should be four—

"It's going to burn." My sister drums her fingers on the counter.

No time for formulas. I am going to have to give this one my best guess. I lift the pan and gently shake it. Forward and back. Side to side. I lower my arm, give my sister a final smirk of superiority, and jerk my hand upward. We have liftoff! The crepe flies two . . . three . . . four . . . feet into the air. The trajectory is perfect. It floats skyward like a creamy, cirrus cloud and then . . .

Splick. Crepe Number Seven sticks to the ceiling. I hold the pan out, waiting for gravity to rescue me. Nothing happens.

"Looks like it hit on the wet side," says Sammi, twisting her lips. "I wonder what kind of luck *that* brings?"

"I will be lucky if Mom doesn't kill me."

"I think we should call *this* recipe Crepes Jorgianna." My sister giggles, which makes me giggle, too, and pretty soon we are in hysterics.

". . . sure, that's all right." Mom strolls into the kitchen, on her cell phone.

"Let's see how long it takes for Mom and Dad to notice," I whisper to Sammi.

"Okay, but when it comes down, you're going to have to explain it."

"*If* it comes down," I say, and we are off on another giggling spree.

"Thanks so much." Mom is waving at us to pipe down. "Bye." She puts her phone on the table. "Something smells heavenly in here."

"I couldn't have said it better myself," I say, our eyes rolling upward.

My sister smacks my shoulder as if she is mad, but then uses me as a shield to hide her giggles. "When did Dad say he'd be here?"

"Actually, that was Mrs. Kondracki."

My sixth-grade teacher? I straighten and stop laughing. "Well?"

The corners of her lips tweak upward. "You'll be starting middle school after spring break."

"Yes!" I twirl to throw my arms around Sammi, but she steps back and all I hug is air. Sammi looks like she wants to flip me in the air like we did with the crepes.

"Al . . . already?" gasps Sammi. "You said Jorgianna wouldn't skip a grade until next year . . . when I would be in high school."

"I know, but Mrs. Kondracki said everyone is in agreement there's no reason to wait," says Mom. "Jorgianna is more than ready academically, and moving her up in the spring gives her the chance to settle in. It's really the best thing."

"For *her*." A red splotch appears on each of Sammi's cheeks. "Doesn't anybody care about what's best for me?"

"Of course we do, sweetie."

It is a lie. From the very beginning, this was about

me—my intelligence, my test scores, my social skills, my emotional well-being. I didn't hear anybody talk about how the jump would affect my sister, except to point out that it would be an added bonus to have her there to help *me* ease into things.

"Can't I have one thing that is all mine?" cries Sammi. "Just for a while? It's only three more months."

"I won't get in your way, Sammi," I say. "You won't even know I'm there."

"Won't even know you're there? Are you serious?" She motions to my pink-and-orange tee, turquoise tights, and green socks. "Look at you! You look like a giant flower, and it's not even a school day!"

That fires up my temper. "I'd rather be a flower than boring old dirt any day."

"Dirt? You'd better take that back—"

"Hey, if the mud fits—"

"Girls," says our mother, "let's calm down and discuss—"

"No!" Sammi backs away. "I don't want to calm down, and I especially do not want to discuss it. I don't want to discuss anything with anyone in this family ever again!" She storms toward the door. Trying to take a wide path around our mother, Sammi cuts the corner too closely and bumps her arm into the granite countertop. We hear the sharp crack of bone against stone. I cringe. Sammi moans but does not slow down.

After my sister is gone, I look at my mother. "Mom?"

"I know, I know."

Sammi has only heard part of the story. If she had a major meltdown over this bit of news, what will she do when she hears the rest of it?

Splat.

Behind me, Crepes Jorgianna Number Seven has returned to Earth.

Lucky me.

FOUR

Moonbeam

"SAMMI?" HER VOICE IS MUFFLED THROUGH MY bedroom door.

I don't answer.

"May I come in?"

Facedown on my bed, I think, *Read the sign, Jorgianna. For once, can't you read the stupid sign?*

After racing upstairs up to my room and before slamming the door behind me, I flung the second hand on my wheel to point to *Sammi Wants to be Alone*. Not that my sister, or anybody else around here, ever pays attention to it. Exhibit A has been camped outside my room for the past twenty minutes.

She taps on the door. "Say something so at least I know you're alive."

I will not. Why should I? I have no say in this family anyway, so what's the point of saying anything to anyone? In protest, I should stay mute until they agree to keep Jorgianna in elementary school. That would show them!

"Come on, Sammi. Why won't you talk to me?"

You're the one with the genius IQ. Figure it out for yourself.

I know it's mean, but I want Jorgianna to feel, if only for a little while, the way I feel *all* the time. Locked out. Left behind. Helpless.

I grab my phone and text Eden. I tell her my world is shattering and to please text me right away. She doesn't text back. I stare at the phone for five minutes, which becomes ten minutes, then fifteen.

I text again.

Eden, where are you? Mondo crisis happening here!

I get nothing in return.

Eeeee-eerkk.

It's the squeaky floorboard in the hall between our

rooms. Jorgianna has surrendered her post. A small victory, I suppose. Except I don't feel victorious. What I feel is crummy.

Yes! We have a ringtone. Finally, a message from Eden!

No!

It's a text from my sister.

Should I read it? No, I won't. I ought to turn off my phone right now and put it away so I won't be tempted to give in, but what do I do instead? I open the text.

Please come out and eat our crepes. I didn't mean to call you dirt. I am sorry to the tenth power. You know what a temper I have. I am also sorry for moving up in school. I am sorry for everything. Love, Jorgianna

I sigh.

It's not her fault she's brilliant. But how come every time something good happens to her, it means something bad has to happen to me? Rolling onto my back, I throw my pillow over my face. My life in middle school wasn't perfect. It wasn't everything I wanted it to be, but at least it was mine.

Was.

*

I hear a sound. Far away. A soft beat. Familiar. My eyes flutter. The room is dark. My head is hanging off the side of the bed. My pillow is on the floor. Is that dried drool on my chin? Yuck. I move my neck and a cramp zaps my skull.

How long have I been asleep?

The scent of warm maple syrup and peaches awakens my hollow stomach. Someone is on the other side of the door. Jorgianna? Mom, probably. She has a thing about not skipping meals. I reach to turn on the light, but pull back. My mom will tell me not to worry; that everything will work out if I only go with the flow. That's her favorite saying: Go with the flow. It is my least favorite saying. Going with the flow usually means I get knocked off my feet by the current and sucked under by a riptide. I close my eyes so I can pretend to be asleep if she, too, ignores the sign, which she will.

Two knocks. Ah, that was the sound.

I try to send a telepathic message to whomever it is, Jorgianna or my mom.

Go away. Leave Sammi alone. Go away. Leave Sammi alone.

"Moonbeam?"

I sit up. "Dad?" I am Moonbeam. Jorgianna is Sunbeam. I have no complaints. I'd rather be a peaceful, mysterious orb than a blinding ball of light that gives you skin cancer any day.

"Permission to enter?" he asks.

"Granted." I turn on my white hyacinth-flower desk lamp.

He sets the plate of crepes on my nightstand. They smell yummy. "You must be starving."

"Nope, not hungry," I snap, a second before my stomach betrays me with a giant *rrrrrrow*.

My dad pretends he didn't hear that and sits on the edge of my bed. "You okay?"

"Not really."

"I'm sorry we didn't tell you there was a chance Jorgianna would be moving up to the middle school ahead of schedule. I honestly didn't think it would happen—"

"You still should have told me."

"I know. Big shock, huh?"

"The worst. It's not too late to say no, is it?"

"Say no?"

"Yeah, let's say no and wait until next year like we planned. What's wrong with that?"

"Nothing, but . . ."

"Jorgianna comes first." I wrap my arms around my knees and hug them to my chest.

"What I was going to say was, *but* it's important not to ignore the input from Jorgianna's teacher and the counselors."

"And my opinion doesn't count."

"Sammi, quit adding things onto my sentences."

"Sorry, but they're all true," I mumble into my knees.

My dad rakes his fingers, streaked with white paint, through his red hair. "Your opinion matters. We love you, too. We're concerned about how you'll adjust too. That's why we haven't rushed things. You know as well as I do that your sister could have skipped grades long before now, but we wanted to make sure you were *both* ready. Your well-being matters to us too, Moonbeam."

I want to believe him, but that tiny word that keeps popping up at the end of *his* sentences stops me. *Too*. Every time he says it, it scratches my heart.

Your well-being matters to us *too*.

We're concerned about how you'll adjust *too*.

We love you *too*.

I am second place. Jorgianna is the star. She could be a scientist and discover a cure for cancer. She could be an attorney and argue a case before the Supreme Court. She could even become president of the United States. Jorgianna will do something incredible with her future. I will probably end up as her personal assistant, getting her coffee and walking her dogs and begging her to wear clothes that match. For the rest of my life, I will be my sister's "too."

Wait a second.

Wait.

One.

Second.

Did my father say . . . ?

Goose bumps ripple up my spine.

"Dad?"

"Yeah?"

"You said 'grades.'"

His eyes widen in panic.

I have him now. "You said Jorgianna could have skipped *grades* long before now."

"You caught that, huh?" He is fidgeting, like he's got an ant down his shirt.

I jump up from the bed. "Are you saying that Jorgianna and I . . . that we . . . ?"

"Yes." I clamp my hands over my ears, but cannot shut out the words—the terrible, terrible words. "Jorgianna isn't skipping one grade, Moonbeam. She's skipping two. You're going to be classmates."

FIVE

Finding Love in the Romance Section (Where Else?)

"BANANA, CAN I COME LIVE WITH YOU AND ARTHUR?" I rub my elbow, still sore from where I banged it on the counter last night.

Hazel eyes glance up from the back of a crime novel. The pale skin around them wrinkling like tissue paper. "It can't be so bad, Sammi, that you're ready to move in to a retirement condo with an old lady and her asthmatic cat."

"You're not old." I tap the ends of the books until all of the spines in the outer row line up perfectly. I empty my lungs. "But it *is* bad."

"You must be referring to Jorgianna's jumping a grade," says my grandmother.

"Newsflash: not one grade. *Two.*"

"Oh goodness! That *is* news."

"Morning, ladies." Mr. Trout, the head librarian, waves a muscular arm from across a sea of paperbacks. "Looking for anything in particular?"

"Just browsing, Norm," says Banana.

"Let me know if I can help," says Mr. Trout.

"Will do." Banana ruffles her short flame-red hair. Streaks of gray shoot out from the temples every which way. Is she blushing?

The maple tree–lined park next to the public library is beginning to fill up, but it's not yet so packed that people are elbowing each other to reach the books they want. That'll change soon. The Tonasket Public Library's spring book sale is a big deal in our town. People show up with book bags, baskets, backpacks, boxes, pillow cases, even luggage carts. Everyone leaves in his/her own good time, juggling, dragging, scooting, or wheeling their literary loot behind them. My grandmother and I have been coming to the sale together since before I knew my ABCs. Normally my yellow floral book bag would be weighted down with all kinds of treasures by now. But today it's empty. It's hard to think about fiction when reality is disintegrating around you.

Banana waits until Mr. Trout is out of earshot to ask, "When?"

"She starts at TMS next week."

"Do you want to talk about it?"

I know whatever I tell my grandmother is sacred, so I spill the ugly details, then plead for help. "What do I do, Banana?"

"Well—"

"I might as well forget about trying to hold orbit in the fourth ring of Saturn. I'll probably be banished from the solar system entirely."

"If it were me—"

"And what if Eden decides to dump me too? I won't have a best friend at Tonasket anymore. I'll get stuck eating with Lauren and Hanna, unless they reject me too. Wouldn't that be awful? Nobody will talk to me and I'll get so depressed I'll have to transfer schools."

"I think you should—"

"What if I get so depressed I can't even get out of

bed to go to my new school? I could get a tutor. No, that's too expensive. Mom and Dad will never go for that. Will they let you do the eighth grade online?"

"Samantha!"

"What?"

"Don't you think you might be overreacting? Just a little? Do you honestly think Jorgianna is out to embarrass you, or herself, at her new school?"

Geez! Isn't anybody on my side? Even Eden said she didn't see what the big deal was about Jorgianna coming up to *our* grade level. Eden has three older brothers and a younger sister, so I guess she's used to everyone overlapping onto everyone else. Of course, she doesn't have a sister like mine. Nobody does. Banana was my last hope. If she won't help me, I'm in trouble. I can't leave home. I'm not runaway material. I'd never survive without a hot shower every day and my detangling conditioner.

Banana leans in. "Maybe you could give it a week or two before hiding under your covers?"

I deflate. "I'll try." What else can I say?

"Good girl." She puts an arm around my shoulders. She smells like white lilacs. All my life she has smelled like white lilacs. I let her lead me across the dewy, sun-dappled grass, even though I know where we are heading.

I turn to her. "What if—?"

"Don't do it, Sammi. Don't 'what if' yourself into a frenzy or you'll never have peace. If I had let all the 'what ifs' my mind created overwhelm me, I wouldn't have done half of the things I've done in my life."

She may have a point. I don't know very many grandmothers that learn to hang glide at age sixty eight. I have the pictures to prove it. Folding my arms across my body, I hug my gray blazer closer. "I have a feeling it's going to be a long spring."

"I have no doubt you will rise to the challenge with your usual grace and charm."

"It's not a beauty pageant, Banana. It's the eighth grade. It's like prison, only with teachers. And band."

She laughs. I wish I was kidding.

As we stroll across the grass, there is one detail about last night I do not confess to Banana. I don't tell her that although I tried to hold out, I ate the crepes my dad had brought to my room—devoured them was more like it. I was so hungry, I couldn't help it. The gooey sweetness of warm peaches wrapped in a fluffy pancake and drizzled with syrup was pure melt-in-my-mouth bliss. The sprinkling of my finely chopped walnuts gave it exactly the right amount of crunch. Wouldn't you know it? Crepes Jorgianna was pure perfection. Dang.

We arrive at our destination. I tip my head sideways to read titles like *Destiny's Hope* and *The Lonely Heart* written in 3-D Victorian script. Ew. I hate romance books. Banana loves them. I don't get these kinds of novels. For one thing, what's up with the weird cover art? Most have heroes with bulging biceps and heroines with smooth shoulders, but hardly anyone ever has a head. A lucky few get a chin or, if they are really fortunate, a nose, but that's it. Romance books aren't my thing. I am into fantasy and apocalyptic thrillers with an occasional mystery thrown in. I have nothing against love, but I would rather have it happen in real life at least once before I have to compare myself to the decapitated women on the romance covers. Banana picks up a book with a sparkly sapphire-blue cover by someone named

Stormy St. Cloud. Yeah, like that's her real name. I will give her some credit, though. This novel, at least, has two complete people, heads and all. Banana puts the book into her straw book bag, then leans over to me to whisper, "I think we are under surveillance."

"Huh?"

"To your left and slightly behind you. In the sports section. A boy is pretending to read a book, but he hasn't taken his eyes off you since we walked over here."

"Oh, Banana." She always thinks boys are looking at me when they aren't. Still, I slowly swivel my neck, because there's always the hope that one day, one glorious day, she might be right. My breath catches in my throat.

It's him! SGB is standing less than twenty feet away. He's wearing jeans and a long-sleeved burgundy waffle tee with the sleeves pushed up. He's slowly flipping the glossy pages of a big book on baseball. Banana is right. His dark brown head is bent, but his green eyes are tracking this direction. I swing back around, and she is quick to read the truth on my face.

"You know him." It's not a question.

"His name is Noah Whitehall. He's in my grade at school."

"You like him." Another statement.

"Shhhh. Not so loud."

"By the way he is staring, I'd say he likes you."

I desperately want her to be right, but if she is, what do I do? The possibilities pile up in my head like a chain-reaction car accident. Is it okay for me to like Noah, even when I know he likes someone else? Especially when that someone else happens to be the most popular girl in school? I need to go outside and get some fresh air. Oh, right, I *am* outside. I force myself to take a deep breath. There's only one way I can think to handle this. "Let's go, Banana. I'm getting hungry. Are you hungry? I think we should go."

"Of course. Lead on, my girl."

I take off, blazing a path through the crowd.

Thud.

Spinning, I see my grandmother on one knee. She is picking up the books she has deliberately dropped in front of the cutest boy in the eighth grade. Noah is bending to help her. I should have known. Banana gave in far too easily. I have no choice but to backtrack.

Blood rushing to my face, I bend down beside her. "You okay?" I ask, though we both know the answer.

"Yes, dear, I'm all right. Lost my grip, is all. Wasn't it nice of this young man to stop and lend a hand? Thank you so much."

"You're welcome," Noah says to her, though he is looking at me. "Hi, Sammi."

My heart flutters faster than a hummingbird's wings. "Hi . . . Na . . . Noah."

Did I just call him Na-Noah?

Banana sits back proudly on her heels and says sweetly, "You know each other?"

"We go to school together," I say, turning my head so she is the only one who can see my I-know-what-you're-up-to smirk. I turn back. "Noah, this is my grandmother, Brooke-Ann Farthington."

"Nice to meet you," he says politely.

"A pleasure."

I slide under the table to get one of Banana's way-ward books. Reaching for it, I am careful not to get grass stains on my jeans. I scoot back out, get to my feet, and discover my grandmother is halfway across the park, speed-walking like an Olympic athlete.

Subtle, Banana.

"Uh . . . she said she saw a friend over by the *National Geographics*," Noah says with a shrug. "She asked me to tell you to meet her at the car in a half hour."

"Thanks."

I wipe some damp grass from the side of my boot. Noah flicks the wave of bangs out of his eyes.

A robin chirps. A car horn beeps. A big guy in a Seattle Mariners jacket releases a sneeze that hits a 9.0 on the Richter scale.

Don't stand there. Do something. Say something!

"Great book sale."

Oh brother.

"Sure is." Noah bobs his head.

I bob my head.

We are having a bobblehead moment. Lovely. I spot a red-and-black paperback lying on its side at the edge of the flower bed. I lunge for it at the exact same moment Noah dives for it too. Clunking heads, we latch on to the book and bring it up together.

"Sorry," he says, rubbing his forehead. "You okay?"

"Uh-huh." This is one time when having a jungle of hair is an advantage. "You?"

"No damage."

I giggle. "This conversation sounds familiar."

He chuckles too.

I glance down, and my laughter trickles to a chipmunk squeak.

Oh no!

The most gorgeous boy in the eighth grade and I are both holding on to a book with a man and woman kissing on the cover. Scrawled across the top in raised gold letters the title reads *Their Secret Love*.

Strike me now, giant meteorite from space.

Noah yanks his hand away as if the cover was on fire. I shove the book into my bag. What a disaster! Who am I trying to kid? Noah and I are not meant to be. I am not sophisticated or popular enough for someone like Noah. I am no Patrice Houston. I let my head fall forward so he can't see me fighting off the tears. Now is his chance to walk away.

I don't hear anything. Is he gone?

"So . . ." Noah's voice cracks. "You want to walk around until you have to go?"

Did he just . . . ?

Did Noah Whitehall, SGB of the eighth grade, ask me, Samantha Eleanor Tremayne of the fourth ring of Saturn, to walk around the book sale with him?

Yes, yes, he did! Hallelujah! Now, as Eden would say, let's get it together. And remember, whatever you do, do not *make The Face.*

I blink and blink and blink faster than the speed of light until I am sure every last drop of water is gone from my eyes, then I relax my face, tip my head up, and say, "Sure."

Things go a whole lot better when you walk around with someone. When you're moving, you don't have to think of a good question to ask or something funny to say. You can talk about whatever comes into your head, like how you can't help picking the blueberries out of the top of your muffin before you eat it or how you love playing soccer, even though you aren't very good. Working our way through the graphic novels, Noah asks me if I have any brothers or sisters. I hesitate, then say, "A younger sister." I am trying to decide if I should tell him that Jorgianna will soon be going to TMS too, when he says, "Hey, look, a book on how to draw your own graphic novel. That would be kind of cool to do, wouldn't it?"

"Yeah," I say.

"Let's take a look." He opens the cover with his right hand and we lean in together.

Whoa! His left arm is, suddenly, around me, his wrist resting lightly on my left shoulder. I've never had a boy put his arm around me before. I'm not sure what to do. Is it okay to move? What if I do? He might think I don't like him. But if I don't he might think I'm scared or creeped out. Does the arm mean anything? What if it doesn't? But what if it does? And if it does, what exactly does it mean? My head is starting to ache thinking of all the possibilities, but then I remember Banana's advice. I force myself to stop with all the what if-ing. I take a deep breath. Noah takes his arm away, I close the cover of the book, and we move on. He guides me by my elbow. It's not sore anymore from where I banged it. Or maybe it is and I'm too excited to care.

I feel like one of those giant cartoon character balloons in the Macy's parade, being pulled along by a string as I sail above everything and everyone. The view is new and bright and I am wider awake then I have ever been. I'm completely happy. Nothing and no one can ruin it. At least, not today.

SIX

On the Dotted Line

"GIRLS, LET'S GO! WITH THIS RAIN, TRAFFIC INTO the city is going to be a bear. Hey, up there! Jorgianna, did you hear me?"

"Coming, Mom!" I fling open my closet door for a quick check in the full-length mirror. It's worse than I could have imagined. I am wearing the most boring outfit I own: a short-sleeved yellow camp shirt, a pair of khakis, matching tan socks, and tan basket-weave flats with little tassels on the toes. My shirt is the exact color of bunny pee. I know this to be a fact because the last time I wore this was when I helped our seven-year-old neighbor, Paisley Wilcox, clean out her rabbit's cage.

Mr. Hoppy decided to take a leak on me, and the pee blended in perfectly. The only good thing I can say about this shirt is that it's clean. I really hate the pleats near the collar with the red zigzag stitching. I look about Paisley's age in this thing too—not a good sign for an eleven-year-old on her first day of eighth grade.

I mess up my short blond hair as hard as I can with both hands. It helps, but it's not enough. Without bright colors, feathers, glittery clips, or spikes, I look like a zombie. How does Sammi manage to look so beautiful in a plain tee and jeans? I look lifeless. I feel as awful as I look. Still, if dressing this way is what it takes to get my sister to end the silent treatment, I suppose it's a small price to pay. Well, it's a big price to pay for someone who adores fashion, but it's worth it. Sammi is barely speaking to me. Having your little sister suddenly show up at *your* school in *your* grade is the stuff of nightmares. I'm hoping once she realizes I'm not going to destroy her world, she'll snap out of it. Then I can go back to dressing normally. I wish she would realize it soon. These pants itch.

"Girls! *Now!*"

A billowing red flag of hair sails past my door. I

grab my charcoal-and-black striped fleece jacket and dark turquoise backpack and race after my sister. Sammi is wearing a copper-colored cardigan over a long white Oxford shirt, black leggings, and black ankle boots. Yawn. I wish she'd put more effort into her wardrobe, but this probably isn't the best time to offer any fashion advice.

Once we are settled side by side in the back of the car and Mom is backing out of the driveway, I try again. "Sammi?" I whisper. She is tracing raindrops on the window, but I know she hears me. "Look, my hair is all blond today and I'm wearing tan."

She nods but doesn't look.

"I've got on loafers, too."

"That's nice."

"Please don't be mad at me."

"I'm not mad," she clips, which means, of course, she *is* mad.

"We can't change what's happened, so why don't we try to make the best of it?"

Her fingertip keeps following the jerky path of a raindrop down the window.

"Come on, Sammi, you can't ignore me forever."

Her head pops up. Turning toward me, she says thoughtfully, "Why not?"

"Huh?"

"You know, that might actually work." My sister starts rummaging through her backpack. "That's what we'll do, Jorgianna. It's a great idea."

"What is?"

Sammi pulls out a pen and a spiral notebook. As Mom drives down Edgemont Avenue, my sister opens the notebook and starts scribbling. "We don't have much time," she mutters to herself.

I bend my neck at an awkward angle to try to read what she is writing. "What are you doing?"

"Making a contract." She never takes her eyes off the page.

"A contract? For us?"

"Uh-huh. We'll make an agreement that while we are both on school grounds we won't talk to, write, call, text, or acknowledge each other."

"You're kidding—"

"We'll each lead our own lives, completely separate in every way. This way you won't step on my toes and I won't step on yours. It's the perfect solution."

I want to say, "No, Sammi, it's not the perfect solution at all. It's an awful idea. What if I get lost? What if nobody talks to me? What if I need you?" I don't, though. I don't say anything. At least she's speaking to me. I don't want to make her angry again.

Our mother is signaling left to turn in to the Tonasket Middle School parking lot. "We've got to hurry," says Sammi. She hands the notebook and pen to me. "Sign, please." She has written her full name near the bottom of the page in her loose, loopy, writing: *Samantha Eleanor Tremayne*. She is waiting for me to do the same. If signing the thing is what it takes to make her happy, I guess it'd be all right. I slowly sign my name next to hers, using my best slanted handwriting. Every letter is the exact same size. *Jorgianna Miriam Tremayne*. I finish as the wheels of our car come to a stop near the curb in front of the school.

"Great. I'll make a copy for you when we get home," says Sammi, shutting the notebook and stuffing it into her backpack. "Oh, and that includes the bus, too. No sitting together, okay?"

"Okay," I say sadly.

She catches Mom eyeing us in the rearview mirror and whispers, "I'll go in first."

I say loudly, "You go ahead, Sammi. I want to talk to Mom for a minute."

Sammi gets out of the car.

Mom gives her a wave. "Bye, sweetie. Enjoy your day."

"I will *now*," she says, smiling at me for the first time in days. She shuts the door and strolls away.

It's all I can do not to shout, "Wait, Sammi, please wait for me!"

My mother turns in her seat. "I know it's forbidden for a parent to set foot on middle school territory, so I won't walk you to the counseling office."

"Thanks, Mom." I lean forward. "You double-checked, right? You made sure I don't—"

"You don't have any classes with Sammi. I'm not certain about lunch, though. I forgot to ask about that."

"You forgot? Moooom, how could you forget?"

"Sorry, honey. I've had a lot on my plate."

Sammi and I in the same lunch? This could ruin everything. I tell myself to calm down and think it through logically. How many kids are in one lunch? One hundred? Maybe two hundred. I don't know. I can't figure the probability without knowing the variables. Okay, I will have to wing it. If it *does* happen and I *do* see Sammi, I will simply turn and head in another direction. I hope she won't be upset if we end up in the same lunch. I don't want her blaming me for it.

My mother sees the concern on my face. "Everything's going to be fine, Jorgianna. You're going to handle your schoolwork beautifully, and Sammi will come around. You'll see." She puts a hand on my shoulder. "Relax. Be yourself."

Be myself? *Be myself?* She cannot mean that. Being myself is how I ended up a friendless freak in elementary school.

"You won't be on your own," says Mom. "Miss Thatcher told me all new students are paired with another student for the first few days. You'll have someone to eat lunch with and give you a hand with your locker, that sort of thing. Isn't that nice?"

I wonder what kind of trouble that girl—please let it be a girl—got into to end up stuck dragging the new kid around. Whoever she is, once she hears about how I got here, she'll despise me too. I open the car door and step into sunshine—the rain stopped. There is light, which I am grateful for, but no warmth, which I could really use. My hands have turned to icicles.

"Text me at lunch if you want—uh-oh, Sammi left her phone." The window slides down and she thrusts out an arm. "Give this to her, will you?"

"Oh . . . I . . . uh . . . you know, I probably won't even see her."

"You might. Take it anyway." It's not a request.

Squinting against the sunlight that peeks between thick fir branches, I watch our car roll out of the parking lot. Once it is out of sight, I turn to face the two-story red-brick building. I take my time shuffling up the sidewalk that funnels into the main walkway. I make sure not to step on the cracks. Kids pass me on both sides. They are in pairs, laughing and talking, too busy to notice someone new. My breath leads the way, hovering in little clouds in front of my nose. I stop in front of a concrete sign that reads TONASKET MIDDLE SCHOOL. So this is it. This is what I've worked for. Begged for. Hoped for. It's a new start at a new school with new people. I should be excited, and I am, but I am also scared. What if it isn't better? What if it's worse?

I hate my pants.

SEVEN

Warning: Universe Collapse Imminent

THE SECOND I WALK INTO FIRST PERIOD, I REGRET IT.

Ting-ting-ta-ting-ting-tong!

I want to do a three-sixty and charge for the door, but it's too late.

"Sammi!" Miss Fleischmann calls out from behind a bunch of upside-down clay planters lined up on her desk. A pink-and-purple tie-dyed bell sleeve swings. "Happy Wednesday, sister of the quarter moon."

"Right back at ya, Miss Fleischmann."

"Take your seat." She points a driftwood drumstick in the direction of my desk. "Close your eyes. Let the music give rise to your creative muse."

Tong-tong-ta-tong-tong-ting. Tong-tong-ta-tong-tong-ting.

The only thing this noise is giving rise to is the Honey Nut Cheerios I had for breakfast. Eden is sitting sideways in her desk, legs outstretched. She has her eyes closed, but the crease between her eyebrows reveals she is enjoying the "music" about as much as I am. I step over two crossed ankles in black tights to get to my desk, behind hers.

My best friend opens an eyeball. "Isn't there some rule that forbids teachers from torturing us?"

"Unfortunately, no."

"I didn't mind the didgeridoo, but the plant pots are on a whole new level."

Ting-ting-ta-ting-ting-tooooong.

I wince. "Go to your happy place, sister of the quarter moon."

"I'd rather go to the nurse's office. I'm getting a headache."

"I'm with you."

Truth is, we like our language arts teacher, even if she is two notches past strange. Miss Fleischmann is big on environmentalism, which is cool. She raises sheep so she can spin the wool into yarn and knit her own clothes, which is also cool. She makes her shoes out of recycled materials, which I *thought* was cool, until it occurred to me I will be stuck listening to her clomp around the room in old detergent bottles for the rest of the year. Miss Fleischmann is always on some kind of weird vegetable juice kick. Last week it was kale juice. I thought kale was some kind of fish until Jorgianna clued me in that it's similar to cabbage, but with super wrinkly leaves. Who knew?

Jorgianna.

I glance at the clock above the door. My sister ought to be in her first period class now too. I wonder if she is nearby. I hope she'll make some friends. Her off-the-charts IQ has a tendency to scare other kids. And teachers. And pretty much everyone. I hope someone gives her a chance.

I giggle. What was with those khaki pants Jorgianna was wearing? And nobody wears tassels on their flats anymore. Where *did* she get those shoes? Banana, prob-ably. I know she was trying to tone her style down for me, but that outfit was sad. I guess it wouldn't kill me to give her a break. Everybody in her life—Mom, Dad, Mrs. Kondracki, Mrs. Vanderslice—has been pushing her pretty hard. I am the only one who doesn't pressure her to work harder, do better, and go further. I will talk to her tonight. I'll make popcorn and we'll have a good long chat about how to survive the middle school universe.

Charlie Twitchell slides into the desk behind me. He cuts a hand through thick wheat-blond hair. "I never thought I'd miss that didgeridoo."

"Only two minutes until the bell."

"Hurry up, bell," he says, taking a pack of cinnamon gum out of his pocket.

Miss Fleischmann lets us chew gum in class, as long as we don't chomp like cows and none of the gum ends up on the desks, floor, walls, or somebody else. Charlie offers a stick to me.

"Thanks." I take one.

Charlie pushes a stick of gum into his mouth, then flattens out the shiny silver wrapper on his desk. Charlie has an origami habit. He's always turning gum and candy wrappers into miniature airplanes and cars.

I ask him, "How's your fairy tale coming along?"

"Slowly. I'm about half done. Yours?"

"I'm stuck on the ending." I take out my three-ring language arts binder. "I'm writing about a girl who becomes a sea horse to save humanity."

"A sea horse? That's cool."

"It's my favorite animal. I go to the Point Defiance Aquarium whenever I can to take pictures. They have a new sea horse exhibit. It has magnified windows so you can find the sea horses in the grasses."

"Magnified, huh? They must be really tiny." Charlie's nose is an inch from the desk as he carefully folds in one corner of the rectangular wrapper.

"They are. Some are barely half an inch long. I like the way they grip the grass with their tails. Did you know a seahorse has no stomach?"

He shakes his head.

"They have to eat constantly to stay alive," I say.

"I guess that's one thing we have in common. My mom says I eat constantly too," says Charlie, shifting his eyebrows.

Grinning, I hand him my gum wrapper so he can fold it into something interesting. Swiveling to face the front of the class, I rest my chin in my hands. I realize I am chewing my gum in rhythm to Miss Fleischmann's *tings* and *tongs*. The noise isn't so bad once you get used to it. Still, it's a relief when the bell rings.

"What were you talking about with Charlie?" asks Eden.

"He thinks he's a sea horse."

She gives me an odd look but doesn't press it.

After she takes roll, Miss Fleischmann announces, "I've got your creative writing journals to hand back."

As a tie-dyed sleeve reaches for a stack of notebooks, I chomp my gum harder. I've gotten Bs on every single writing assignment this semester. Sometimes a B-plus, sometimes a B-minus, but always a B.

B for blah.

Our last assignment was to develop a fictional character. I came up with a long list of things my character likes—favorite foods, music, songs. I wrote about the kinds of clothes she likes to wear and even what she carries in her purse. I sooooo want an A in my writing journal.

A for amazing.

Please, let me get an A. Just one little, itty-bitty, teen-weeny, pointy-hatted A.

"Some of you did an outstanding job on your characters, but some of you need to spend more time on your writing," says Miss Fleischmann, pushing back her rolled blue bandana hair band. "When you rush, it shows."

I sit taller. Not me. I didn't rush at all. Miss Fleischmann glides down our row. She's wearing her moccasins today, so it's eerily quiet. She places my black spiral notebook on my desk without looking at me, so I can't tell if she liked it or not. I take a deep breath and flip through the pages—slowly at first, then faster and faster and faster until I get to the last entry . . .

Ugh. Another blah B. I know Miss Fleischmann's comments are on the next page. I am in no mood to see them. Maybe later. I close my notebook. I don't want to know. Yes, I do. I open the book. I slide the pages past me until I come to the last one that has writing on it.

A good start, but writing about favorite movies and songs only skims the surface of your character. Deep down, who is she? Is she happy with her life? What are her fears? Her dreams? I don't feel I truly know what makes her tick. Do you?

Guess not.

Shading my paper, I glance over my shoulder. Charlie has lifted the first page and is reading his comments on the second page. He got an A-minus.

Another glimpse ahead. Eden's paper is decorated with a swirling A.

Errrrgh!

I slam my journal shut for the last time. What am I doing wrong? I tried so hard this time and what did it get me? Another blah B. Maybe trying doesn't have anything to do with it. Maybe you are either a good writer or you aren't.

After Miss Fleischmann hands back our journals, she continues where we left off yesterday, discussing fairy tales. She talks about fairy tales from other countries and cultures. I try to take notes, but as the period winds down I realize I have hardly written a thing. There's a long line of cursive As down the page and not much else.

"Don't forget," says Miss Fleischmann, "your fairy

tales are due next Monday, then we'll be starting the poetry unit."

A chorus of groans echoes through the room, mine included. Something tells me I am going to be no better at writing poetry than fiction.

"Roses are red, violets are blue," I hear Charlie's voice in my ear. "Some poems rhyme, some poems don't."

I giggle. Charlie is hilarious, but I have to be careful because his sense of humor usually gets me into trouble. Miss Fleischmann rarely sees the comedian (Charlie). She only sees the audience (me) laughing her head off. Charlie does a wicked Chewbacca roar and a perfect Mr. Simonton, right down to the way our math teacher coughs up phlegm while we are trying to work a problem. He sounds like an old car that won't start. *Huh-yack-yack-yack. Huh-yack-yack-yack.*

The bell rings. I load up my backpack and follow Eden out of class. We walk past a girl opening her locker, Noah, and a couple of seventh grade boys playfully shoving each—whoa!

Back it up.

Noah?

"Hi, Sammi."

I nearly swallow my gum. My heart starts beating at turbo speed. What is he doing here? Was he waiting for me?

"Hi," I say.

Eden is a glacier. The expression etched onto her face is a mixture of curiosity and disbelief. I did tell her I bumped into him at the book sale last weekend, but I didn't tell her we walked around together. By ourselves. For thirty-three minutes. I wasn't sure if he was off-again or on-again with Patrice. I didn't want Eden to spoil it by telling me they were on-again. I wanted to enjoy that day for what it was, whatever it was, even if what it was was nothing.

"I'm across the hall first period," says Noah. "Where's your next class?"

"B wing. World geography with O'Canlon."

"I've got PE. Want to walk together?"

"Okay." I tap Eden. "See you at lunch?"

"Uh-huh," gulps my still-frozen best friend.

With a small wave I leave her to thaw.

Noah puts his hand on my back, guiding me

through the crowded hallway. I feel like a salmon fighting my way upstream. Eyes track us. I am suddenly aware of every little thing that is not quite perfect—the chips in my coral fingernail polish, the small rip in the seam of my legging, the scuff mark on the toe of my boot. Is this how celebrities feel? We pass a group of seventh grade girls. They giggle and point. I grin. I look at Noah, who is also grinning. Being noticed, really and truly noticed, is new for me. It's kind of fun, like being a princess. I am brimming with confidence. Noah and I turn the corner to B wing and my imaginary crown topples to the floor.

Tanith and Cara are in front of their locker. Cara is the first to see us. She tugs on the belt loop of her friend's jeans, but Tanith is taking off her jacket and is trying to shoo her away. Finally, Tanith turns. Her head comes up. Our eyes meet. Mine widen. Hers narrow. She flings her jacket into her locker. Yanking Cara toward her, Tanith whispers in her friend's ear. Cara is gripping her phone like it's a parachute rip cord. In seconds Patrice will hear the news and know all about Noah and me. But *what* will she know? And shouldn't I know it first? Does Noah like me as much as I like him? He must. It's why he found me after first period, right? I want to ask him if he's going to the dance, but I'm scared. What if he is, but doesn't want to go with me? What if he isn't? Then I'll only embarrass him. I really have to learn to stop with the what ifs.

Noah feels me stiffen. "You okay?"

"Fine."

We are in front of Room B–139.

"See ya, Sammi."

"Noah, wait. I . . . uh . . . I was wondering . . ." the temperature inside my sweater shoots up fifty degrees.

Green eyes peer into mine. "Yeah?"

"I . . . uh . . . was wondering if you . . . I mean, there's a dance coming up and I was just . . . are you going?"

There. I said it!

He tips his head. "Are you?"

I nod.

"Me too," he says.

"Good."

"Good."

"Good."

I think it's his turn.

"I'd better get going or I'll have to endure Rigley's wrath. See ya, Sammi."

My spine tingles when he says my name. "See ya, Noah."

I am sure Mrs. O'Canlon probably taught us some important stuff in geography, but for the life of me I don't know what it was. After third period I drop off my books at my locker and head to the cafeteria, as usual. Eden is waiting for me near the stage, as usual. "Where have you been?"

"Where I always am third period, math—"

"Why didn't you answer any of my texts?"

I grunt. "I left my phone in the car this morning."

"So what's the scoop? Is the gossip going around true? Are Noah and you—?"

"Friends. Officially, we're friends."

"Woooow. Noah likes you. You like Noah. How does that feel?"

I squeal. "Spectacular."

Eden glances at Saturn's cluster of tables and her smile fades. Reality check. We both know what Noah liking me and me liking Noah means. Forget the fourth ring of Saturn. I will never be allowed to orbit remotely anywhere near her again. Strangely enough, this doesn't bother me nearly as much as I expected it to. I guess I'd rather be liked by Noah and ignored by Patrice than the other way around. Of course, there is a price to pay. It will be tough eating lunch without my best friend. We've always been a team. I'm really going to miss Eden, but it's not fair to hold her back. She's worked as hard as I have to reach an inner ring.

"You go on," I say to my best friend, trying to keep my voice level and strong. "Tell Bridget and Stella hi from me."

"Sammi, no! I'm not going to leave you. I can't—"

"It's okay, Eden. Really it is."

"But who will you eat with?"

"I don't know. Maybe Lauren or Hanna. Maybe my sister—"

"That's right! I totally forgot. It's Jorgianna's first day. How's she doing?"

"Okay, I guess. I haven't seen her." I don't mention our contract. Now that I think about it, I don't know why I freaked out so much over my sister coming to TMS. Nothing awful has happened. My universe hasn't collapsed. Banana was dead-on, as usual. If you aren't careful, you really can "what if" yourself into a bad place. "I'll be fine," I say to Eden. "I'll eat with my sister, if it turns out she has our lunch."

"Oh, she has our lunch, all right."

"How do you know?"

Dark eyes widen. "Because she just walked into the cafeteria."

I start to turn, but an arm shoots out. Fingers dig into my wrist. "Sammi, your sister is . . . uh . . . well she's . . . you'd better brace yourself."

"Brace myself? Why?"

Eden swallows hard. "Jorgianna is with Saturn."

EIGHT

To Quote Dr. Seuss

"HERE IT IS," PATRICE SAYS, TWISTING HER WRIST so her palm faces up. "The legendary Tonasket Middle School cafeteria. Big dealy woo, huh?"

The huge battleship-gray room is packed. I've never seen so many kids in one place, and every one of them is in a hurry to get somewhere. The concrete squeals as chair after chair is scooted up to one of the dozens of round tables. Sunlight streams through pockets of glass in the arched ceiling. On the wall next to me someone has painted an enormous roaring tiger with the initials TMS on its collar. Saliva drips from its sharp white fangs.

"It's bigger than the cafeteria at Greenleaf, and the skylights are nice," I say above the noise. "Hey, is that a taco bar? I love—"

"No!" Patrice's sharp tone sends goose bumps up my neck. "No tacos, Jorgianna. Never tacos."

"Oh, okay." She is so determined, I don't dare ask why.

She points to the right. "We usually get salads or veggie burgers at the deli." She points to the left. "Stay away from the soup. The cooks like to get creative. They combine leftovers so you end up with gunk like what they are serving today, the three C special."

"What's the threesy special?"

"Three C," she enunciates. "Cabbage, corn, and clam chowder."

"The deli works for me."

"BTW, it's up to you, Jorgi, but I'd keep quiet about Greenleaf. Word is out that you skipped a couple of grades, and nobody likes a show-off."

Don't I know it. "I won't talk about it," I say.

"Let's drop our stuff," she says. "I'm at the middle table."

"You're the center of the universe." I giggle.

"Exactly," she says without cracking a smile.

I stop short. "Oh!"

"What?"

"Noth . . . nothing. I caught my shoe." The truth is, I have spotted my sister. She is standing near the stage. Her back is to me, but I'd know that flame-red hair anywhere. Eden is opposite her, facing me. I think Eden has seen me, but I'm not sure. I don't want to stare. Fortunately, Patrice leads me to the left, away from Sammi and Eden.

"Speaking of shoes," Patrice shoots me a pained look, "what is with your outfit? I almost didn't recognize you this morning."

"I almost didn't recognize myself," I murmur.

"Good thing I rescued you, or you'd be stuck under the big tiger."

Patrice means I'd be having lunch with Hanna Welch, who is sitting with one of her friends by the tiger mascot on the wall. I'm not sure what is so terrible about that. Hanna was the student Miss Thatcher assigned to show me around. She was friendly. She knew I was Sammi's sister, but didn't fire a bunch of questions at me. Instead, she kept encouraging *me* to ask her any questions I had about the school, my classes, sports, and clubs. Hanna was about to show me where my locker was this morning when Patrice came along and took me away, which reminds me . . .

"Patrice, I still need to find my locker," I say.

"Yeah?"

"I've been up and down every hallway."

"Okay."

"You said you'd help me—"

"And I will. Chill, girl. It can't walk away."

We are strolling toward the middle table, but I notice that every seat there is taken. I am getting jittery. Where are we supposed to sit? As I start to tell Patrice we'd better look for another table, the sea of bodies parts.

"Newbie in the house!" Patrice taps a girl with a side ponytail, who nudges the girl beside her, who flicks the next girl, who slides out of her seat. Waving to me, the girl points to her spot.

"Don't move for me." I edge toward her. "I'll find a spot at another table."

"I'm almost done." She tosses her napkin on her tray, but anyone can see she is not close to being done. There's more than half a salad and a package of unopened string cheese on her tray. The girl next to her is also getting up. Her tray is nearly full too.

"I'm Jorgianna Tremayne."

"Bridget Forrester," says the first girl. "This is Stella Nguyen."

"Hi," says Stella. "We usually sir over there." She points two tables over.

"I know you," I say to Stella. "You're in my science class."

"Yes!" She puts a hand to her cheek. "There's got to be thirty-five kids in Wannamaker's class and I sit on the other side of the room. How did you remember me?"

"I have a—" I am about to tell her I have an excellent memory, but remember my resolve to be as normal as possible. "—I'm into fashion," I sputter, pointing to her plum-colored velvet tee. "Your top is cute."

"Thanks."

"It's a Catinka DeLong, from last summer's jewel-tone collection, isn't it?"

"Yes!"

What am I doing? I *am* a show-off.

"You don't have to move for me," I repeat.

Stella sighs. "Yeah, we do, but it's okay. You seem sweet."

"You sure do." Bridget frowns.

"You're Sammi's sister, right?" asks Stella.

"Yes."

A look passes between the two girls. Is it worry? Sadness? Fear? It happens so quickly I can't be sure.

"We've eaten lunch with your sister," says Stella. "She's super nice."

"Will you tell her that?" asks Bridget, almost apologetically. "Tell her we had fun with Eden and her, okay?"

Am I missing something?

"Sure," I say.

"Jorgi!" Patrice is dragging me backward by the strap of my pack. "You're next to me. Tanith, move your stuff, will you? You're hogging two spots. And why are you eating that cottage cheese with peaches stuff again? That is gross."

"Forgive *meee*," says the girl with the ponytail, rolling her eyes.

"Everybody, this is Jorgi," Patrice calls. "Jorgi, this is Tanith, Cara, Mercy, Desiree—where is India? Oh, there she is. India, do you have a dollar?"

"Sure." A petite brunette girl with an angled, chin-length bob reaches for her purse.

"Hi, hi, hi." I memorize each name and face. "I'm Jorgianna." I don't mean to correct Patrice in front of her friends, but I don't like nicknames.

"Jorgi and I met at the Whitaker Gallery," says Patrice, missing my hint completely. "She won Best in Show in the district art competition."

The girls clap politely.

"Well, you *almost* won," Tanith says to Patrice. "First place in the photography division and second place in the whole entire competition is a pile of amazeballs."

Everyone gives Patrice a big round of applause.

Dang! I should have said something to Patrice about her photograph when I saw her this morning. After she left the art gallery, I went to find her picture. The image was of a little girl at the aquarium. She had curly red pigtails and was wearing a strawberry-pink coat. Her tiny hands were clamped onto the big window of the exhibit. Inside the tank, two arms of a maroon giant Pacific octopus clung to the very same spots on the glass. One large eye looked down at the child, as if wondering, *Who is this strange pink creature?* The photo was sharp, the colors rich and vibrant. Bright-pink coat. Murky-blue water. Deep-red, mottled octopus.

"I thought your photo was incredible," I say to Patrice. "You're a good photographer."

"Thanks," she says.

"My sister loves the PDA. She goes there all the time."

"Huh?"

"The Point Defiance Aquarium. That's where you took the picture, right?"

"Oh . . . right. Sure."

Winning her category meant Patrice had been in the running for Best in Show. In the end, though, she had come in second place. She had lost to me. The moment Mrs. Vanderslice slapped that colossal purple ribbon on my piece, Patrice knew she had lost too, but she hadn't held it against me. She'd still wanted to be friends. I liked that. Sammi was always keeping score. Patrice didn't seem to care at all.

"Come on, Jorgi, let's get lunch," says Patrice. Leading the way to the deli bar, she turns. "You know, now that we're one and two in the district competition, I'll bet they do an article about us in the school newspaper."

"I hope not."

"Really? Why?"

I snicker. "The only thing worse than one show-off is two."

"Maybe. But I think it's better to be a show-off then fade into the background. So this"—she tips her head toward my bunny pee shirt—"this is the real you?"

"No." I tug at the hated collar. "Not even close."

"Then why are you wearing it?"

"My sis—I mean, it's my first day. I thought I should try to fit in." I attempt to toss off a light laugh, but it sounds more like an old helium balloon deflating.

"Be who you are and say what you feel, because those who mind don't matter and those who matter don't mind."

"Dr. Seuss."

"The one and only." Patrice reaches for a plastic container filled with salad greens, tomatoes, and sunflower seeds and puts it on my tray. She gives herself one too. "Do us all a favor, Quirky Chic, and come as yourself tomorrow."

"I will."

"BTW, we meet at the atrium if you want to hang out with us before school."

"Thanks." I start to reach for a peanut butter cookie.

"No, not yet!" cries Patrice. "We always come back for dessert and we only get the chocolate chip cookies."

"Okay." I wonder what she has against peanut butter.

"You will do it, won't you?" she asks.

"Eat only the chocolate chips?"

"No, I mean dress as yourself tomorrow."

I laugh, this time for real. "I will."

It is the easiest and best promise I have ever made.

I get on bus number twelve and take the seat right behind the driver. This way, Sammi has plenty of seats to choose from. She can sit near me or way in the back. I hope she sits close to me, but she probably won't. Sammi doesn't want to have anything to do with me. I lean my forehead against the cool glass and close my eyes.

I am exhausted. Not from my classes, but from trying not to appear too new or too smart or too young or too much of anything that will offend anyone. I feel like one of those shape-shifter aliens in the movies, constantly turning myself into something different to make someone else happy.

I like Patrice's attitude. She's herself and she doesn't apologize for it to anybody. I can tell by the way kids act around her she's popular, but is she popular because she's herself or is she herself because she's popular? I'm not sure, but I admire her strength and independence. I am beginning to think maybe it wasn't my fault I didn't have any friends at Greenleaf. Maybe it was their fault. I'm intelligent. Deal with it. I'm eleven years old. Live with it. I am into fashion. Get over it. I'm done shape-shifting.

The seat bounces. Ugh. I refuse to paint on another smile and chat with anyone else today. I turn both shoulders toward the window to make this clear, but someone is tugging my coat sleeve. "I need to talk to you."

I spin, my eyes flying open. "Sammi!" Could it be true? My sister actually wants to be seen with me?

Her forehead is wrinkled. "How do you know Patrice Houston?"

"Huh?"

"Where did you meet her? Did you go up to her? Did she say anything about me? Did she mention Noah?"

"Who's Noah?"

"Oh, for goodness sake, Jorgianna." She slaps a hand to her forehead and lets her neck fall backward.

The bus driver shut the doors and pulls away from the curb.

"Don't blow a brain cell," I say. "I met Patrice at the art show. *She* came up to *me* and said she liked my sweater. You know, the one you said made me look like a human sombrero?"

Her head still resting on the back of the seat, Sammi slowly turns her neck to look at me.

"She said she wanted to show me an exhibit she liked," I explain. "Guess whose it was?"

Sammi's hand slips off her forehead. "Yours?"

"Yep. I saw her again this morning before school. Miss Thatcher assigned Hanna Welch to show me around, and we were leaving the counseling office when we ran into Patrice. She said she'd take over for Hanna, since the two of us were already friends." A warmth fills me as I remember the way Patrice firmly took my arm, the way she said the word "friend."

"So that's everything?"

"Yes. Well, no."

"No?"

"Bridget and Stella told me to tell you they had fun eating lunch with Eden and you."

She relaxes a little. "They're super nice."

"That's exactly what they said about you." I unzip my backpack. "BTW, you left your cell phone in the car this morning." I hand it to her.

"Thanks."

Now it is my turn to ask questions. "Why the third degree about Patrice?"

Sammi shakes her head. "It's complicated."

"If I can handle advanced algebra, I think I can follow you."

"Life isn't math, Jorgianna."

"It ought to be. Math makes sense."

Sammi scoots closer to me and whispers, "Do me a favor and be careful around Patrice, okay?"

"Careful?" I study her. "Why?"

"Just don't be so gullible. You're too trusting—"

"I know what gullible means. I have an IQ of—"

"This has nothing to do with intelligence," snaps Sammi. "You're in a different world now."

"Different is my middle name, in case you hadn't noticed. Patrice likes different."

"That's not what I meant."

I know. What Sammi meant is I have never had a real friend before, so I don't know how to be one.

"Jorgianna, I don't want you to get caught up in my . . ." Sammi trails off.

"Your?"

"It's . . . it's complicated."

"You said that already. I may not be as beautiful or popular as you are, Sammi, but I think I can choose my own friends."

"I didn't say you couldn't—"

"Then leave me alone."

"I'm only trying to help," says Sammi.

Now? She wants to help me *now*? Where was she today when I couldn't find my locker? Or when I got lost in D wing? Or had to borrow a towel from Julia in PE because nobody told me I would need one on my first day of school? My head is spinning and I can feel the lava that is my temper begin to bubble. "You can't tell me what to do anymore, Sammi. Our lives at school are totally and completely separate because you wanted it that way. You don't step on my toes and I don't step on yours, remember?"

"Okay, I admit I might have gone a little overboard with that this morning."

"You think?"

"Take it easy, will you?" She looks around to see if any of the other kids on the bus are listening.

"Don't tell me to take it easy."

"Temper, Jorgianna," she says, which doesn't help.

I am hungry. I am tired. And for the past eight hours, I've been stuck in this awful forest-ranger uniform. I am in no mood for a lecture. "You shouldn't even be sitting here," I say. "We have a contract, remember?"

"Fine." The word snaps my ear like a rubber band. "You're on your own. Good luck."

"Keep your luck."

Sammi pops out of her seat and heads to the back of the bus.

Seven minutes later we are at our corner. The bus driver pulls the lever that flips the stop sign out from the side of the bus. Red lights flash. I trot down the ridged steps of the bus. The moment my feet touch smooth cement I take off. It's the one thing I *can* do in these dumb shoes—run.

"Jorgianna, wait!"

She is too late. I am already in full stride. The tears welling in my eyes blur the path in front of me. I stumble on a cracked piece of sidewalk, but I don't fall. I will *not* fall. And I will *not* cry. My heavy pack bashing into the back of my shoulder with each step, I let the wind dry my tears as I sprint for home.

Sammi can't catch me.

She never could.

NINE

One Murder, Possibly Two

LIKE ODETTE THE SWAN QUEEN, I PRANCE INTO the kitchen and do a near-perfect ballerina pirouette. I get no response. At the table Sammi is deep into reading the back of the Cheerios box. At the stove my father skates a spatula around a pan of eggs.

Take two. Chin up, shoulders back, I stretch one arm out gracefully as I glide past my father. He glances up. Through the haze of steam, our eyes connect. His lips slide up one cheek, but all he says is, "Morning, Sunbeam."

Hearing my father, Sammi looks up. She drops her

spoon. It makes an ear-splitting *clang* against the ceramic bowl and sprays milk all over her steel-blue sweater. Sammi's mouth is open so wide that if the three black crows bobbing on wires attached to the neon-orange felt Robin Hood hat on my head were real, they would have an unabated flight path to her tonsils. "Jorgianna Miriam Tremayne, you are *not* wearing that to school."

Mission: Fashion Shock and Awe accomplished.

"It appears, dear sister, that I am." I throw my head back, making the three faux blackbirds hovering above me bounce on their little wires. Hands on hips, I strike a pose in my tangerine blouse with five layers of chiffon petals around the neck and bell sleeves the size of sailboat masts. My sister's horrified gaze travels down the frothy blouse, taking in the massive bow that ties at the hip of my black skirt, leggings in a black-and-white diamond harlequin pattern, and a pair of black leather ankle boots with brushed-nickel Pilgrim buckles.

Sammi gasps. "Are those mom's boots? Did she say you could borrow them?"

I ease into my chair. "They are and she did."

My sister grabs a napkin and dabs at her milk-splattered sweater. "I don't believe you. Those boots are way too expensive. She'd never let you—"

"Well, she did."

"Daaaaad!" Sammi sounds like a toddler throwing a tantrum.

Our father sets a plate of scrambled eggs and a piece of toast—cut on the diagonal (exactly the way I like it)—in front of me. He scoots the jar of orange marmalade close to my plate before casually leaning back to inspect my boots.

I stretch out my leg. "Mom said it was fine."

"She's lying," spits my sister.

"I am not."

"You *so* are—"

"I am *so* not. Ask her yourself."

"Okay, okay, girls. Finish your breakfast. I'll check in with your mother for the final word." He chuckles. "It's those birds that worry me, Sunbeam. Be careful, young lady, you don't want to poke someone's eye out."

As our father heads back to the stove, Sammi grumbles, "I should have put something about clothes in the contract."

"Contract?" Dad's head pops up.

"It's a little agreement we made so I don't embarrass her at school," I say.

My sister is giving me the stink eye. "This is your idea of *not* embarrassing me?"

"I'll stay out of your way, but I'm not changing myself for you or anybody else," I say firmly. "From now on, I wear what I want to wear."

"Fair warning—" Sammi glances up at my birds—"you're going to get teased in a big way at school."

"I'll take that risk." I plunge my knife into the marmalade. "A bird must sing its song, even if it is alone in the forest."

"Shakespeare?" asks Dad, passing behind me.

I grin. "Jorgianna."

"You look like a Halloween court jester being attacked by a flock of crows," says Sammi.

"It's not called a flock of crows. It's called a murder."

"I'll say."

"On the upside, you're both dressed in complementary colors," says my dad. His eyes go from my orange blouse to Sammi's blue sweater. "And you know what complementary colors do, don't you?"

"They bring out the best in each other," I say.

"Not this time," growls Sammi. "This could be your worst outfit ever, Jorgianna. I absolutely hate it!"

"I absolutely love it!" screams Patrice when I stroll into the Tonasket Middle School atrium.

The girls swarm me.

"That hat is craze-amaze to the tenth power," squeals Tanith. "Did you make it?"

"Well, I—"

"Where did you get that wicked top?" asks Cara.

"I got—"

"I love your Pilgrim boots, Jorgianna." India jumps in. "Did you get them online at Sweet Feet?"

"These? They're—"

"Are those Get a Leg Up tights?" asks Desiree.

"Actually—"

"Can I borrow your skirt?" asks Mercy. "Please, oh please, oh please—"

"Whoa!" Patrice steps in to wave them back. "Let her finish a sentence, why don't you? Go ahead, Jorgi."

I turn to Tanith. "I didn't make the hat, but I did add the crows and sequin trim." I do not tell her it was one of Banana's thrift store discoveries. I'm not sure if Patrice and her friends are into thrift stores, but based on their clothes, I doubt it. I swing to find Cara. "I got the blouse for Christmas last year from my grandmother, but I picked it out. It's a Leena James top from Nordstrom's." To India I say, "These are Monkey See boots, and I borrowed them from my mom." I wave to Desiree. "I love Get a Leg Up, but these are Stems," and finally, to Mercy, "Sure, you can borrow my skirt." Again, I decide not to reveal that it's yet another treasure from the Helping Hands thrift shop, but I do add, "When I'm not in it, of course."

Everyone laughs.

"I told you she had a killer style," says Patrice, practically bursting with satisfaction.

India digs in her purse. "I want to take a picture of you—oh, poo, I think I left my phone in my locker."

I groan. "I still have to find mine."

Desiree giggles. "Your phone or your locker?"

"My locker."

India stops her search. "You haven't found your locker yet?"

"No."

"What's the number?"

"904."

"904? Isn't that one of the—"

"India, do you have a dollar?" asks Patrice.

"Sure."

"I said I'd help you find your locker, Jorgi," says Patrice. "Girls, let *me* handle this one, okay?" She giggles, though I don't get what is so funny. I suck in my lips to keep from saying this is the third time she has said that and still, I remain lockerless.

"I'll bet it's in G wing," says Tanith, "by the library."

"Or on the other side of the janitor's closet," says Desiree. She nudges Cara, who says, "Right, right. Or it could be near the gym. There's that long bank of lockers near the boys' locker room."

I am rooting for G wing.

"Maybe it's a typo," offers Mercy.

A typo! Why didn't I think of that? And I'm the one with the skyscraper IQ. I check my silver watch with the pearly face. Four minutes until the bell. If I leave now, I'll have enough time to stop in the office and find out if the mystery locker even exists. I am gathering up my stuff when Mercy says, "Uh-oh."

A tall, thin boy in a white long-sleeved tee, jeans, and tennis shoes is marching toward us. His sleeves are pushed up to his elbows. I don't recognize him. He's cute, in a disheveled way. He doesn't seem threatening, yet everyone in my group has the expression of a victim in a horror movie right before the killer's chainsaw comes ripping through the door. Overgrown mahogany hair hangs in angled slices in front of his eyes. He sweeps them aside, and light-green eyes go from one girl to the next to the next. They pause briefly on me as if to say "you are a surprise," but then move on to find his target. "Patrice," he clips. "I need to talk to you."

"Now?"

"Yes. Enough with the texting—"

"Okay, okay." Patrice takes his arm and turns him toward the wall of windows. Glancing at Tanith over her shoulder, she jerks her head and, suddenly, I am being whisked out of the atrium by my friends. They shuffle me out so quickly, I have to throw up a hand to keep my bird hat from going airborne.

"This is it," says Tanith once we reach the hallway.

"I'm not surprised," says Desiree. "It's been coming for a long time."

"Still, it's so sad when it does," says India.

"So, so sad," echoes Mercy.

"What is going on?" I whisper to Cara.

"That's the boy Patrice likes. They're not getting along."

I'd never had a crush before. Most of the boys I knew at Greenleaf Elementary School were annoying. They were always throwing food and paper and rubber bands at you. Plus, they smelled like the inside of old tennis shoes left in the rain. I don't know if the boys in middle school throw less and shower more, but I doubt it.

"It's probably a big misunderstanding," says Mercy. "You know, like all of the other times. I bet they are in there right now working it all out, like all of the other times."

"We can dream," says Cara.

I lean toward Desiree. "Do they do this a lot?"

"About once a week." She bites her lip. "But this time is . . . different."

"Why?"

She doesn't answer me.

India sighs. "It's so sad."

"I'm afraid Tanith is right," says Cara. "It looks like this is the final straw."

"Then we'll have to be incredibly supportive when she comes out," I say.

"Incredibly supportive?" Tanith snorts. "Who says that?"

I open my mouth to snap back, "*I* say that," but hear my sister's voice in my head saying, "Temper, Jorgianna," and I clamp my lips together.

"Jorgi, unfortunately, you're going to be the last person Patrice will want to see," says Mercy.

"Me? Why?"

"Stop doing that," snarls Tanith.

"Doing what?"

"Asking why. You're always asking why. It's soooo annoying."

I'm annoying? Tanith has known me for, what, nineteen hours? How can she say I am *always* doing anything?

I am about to tell her this too, when India pats my arm. "Jorgianna, it's not you . . . it's the whole situation . . . it's all so . . . complicated."

Where have I heard that before?

"Great!" Patrice's voice echoes through the hall. She flies around the corner, barreling straight for us and muttering, "Boys. Idiots. All of them. Boys."

Tanith rushes to meet her. "Are you okay?"

"I'm fantastic," she hits the *t*s so hard little flecks of saliva fly out of her mouth. "Happy as can be." Not slowing her stride, Patrice's icy gaze locks on to me. "Be sure and thank your sister for me, Jorgi."

"My . . . sister?" I bite down, snapping off the "why" a millimeter from the end of my tongue.

"Yes, let's all send a thank-you note to Sammi Tremayne for stealing *my* boyfriend!" Patrice steams past me, stirring up a breeze that sends a chill up me and sets the three little black birds on my hat swaying.

Tanith, India, Cara, Mercy, and Desiree scurry after her.

The slam of the door goes through my entire body. I am alone in the hallway, the hair on my arms still on alert, the little crows above me still trembling. I am not sure what to do. I'd focused so much energy on making sure I didn't spoil Sammi's social life, it never occurred to me that *she* might be the one to ruin *mine*.

TEN

Color Me Shocked

IT'S SATURDAY MORNING AND FOR THE MILLIONTH time I pound on the bathroom door.

"In a minute!" comes the millionth and one reply.

"You said that ten minutes ago. You'd better be in there cleaning, because you're on bathroom duty. Or did you forget about losing our crepe tossing bet?"

"I didn't forget."

I bang on the door again. "Jorgianna!"

"Use Mom and Dad's."

"I don't have to go. I have to talk to you."

"I'm not deaf."

"Eden told me Hanna heard from Stella that Desiree said Patrice flipped out at you last week."

It was exactly what I'd feared. I had a feeling Patrice would take out her anger at me on my little sister. This was all my fault. I should have been straight with Jorgianna and told her everything that first day we rode home on the bus together. I was not about to make the same mistake twice.

I pound again. "Jorgianna, open the door!"

Hinges squeak and suddenly a massive cloud of steam rolls out of the bathroom. I cough and wave it away. The hot fog evaporates and I see my little sister in the two-sizes-too-big jelly-bean print terry cloth bathrobe Aunt Ellen gave her for her birthday. Still trying to grow into it, she's had to wrap the belt twice around her tiny waist. A white bath-towel turban perches on her head. It leans to the left, reminding me of Mrs. Vanderslice's hairdo.

"It's all yours." Bare feet skitter past. "BTW, it's Jorgi."

"What is?"

"My name. From now on, call me Jorgi."

"But you hate nicknames."

"A person can evolve."

Since when is a nickname evolving? "Okay, *Jorgi*," I say, though it feels weird on my tongue. "Tell me what happened—"

"Nothing happened."

"That's not what I heard." I follow the damp footprints to her room. "I heard Patrice yelled at you. I heard she yelled at you about Noah and me."

She pokes through her underwear drawer. "Yelled is a strong word."

"Did she or didn't she yell at you?"

"You mean like you're doing now?"

"Arrrrrgggh!" My sister can be so exasperating.

"If you must know," says Jorgianna, "Patrice was pretty steamed you stole her crush."

"I didn't steal—"

"And she might have taken out her frustration on me when he decided to embarrass her right there in the atrium in front of all of her friends."

I crumple against her doorframe. "He didn't."

"Yes." Grabbing a ball of red socks out of her drawer, she sits on the edge of her bed. "He did."

"He probably didn't know any other way. Patrice is a very . . . uh . . . determined person."

"So you're saying it's Patrice's fault?"

"Yes. No. Partly."

"Multiple choice? You want me to wait while you pick one?"

"Look, the thing you have to understand about Noah and Patrice is . . . see, they don't . . . they're not . . . what I'm trying to say is—"

"It's quite the Gordian knot."

"Huh?"

"Complicated. So very complicated," she says, using her superior-intellect voice. *Grrrrr*. Sometimes it's all I can do to keep from wringing her neck. How do I explain the situation to her? She's too young to understand.

"You can't steal a person's heart, Jorgianna," I say. "They have to give it to you. They have to give it of their own free will. You can't make a person like you or, for that matter, *not* like you. Look, I know you've never had a crush before—"

"How do you know?" Her head snaps up. "You don't know if I've ever had a crush on somebody. You've never bothered to ask."

Her tone stings, but she is right. "Have you?"

She bites her lip as she slowly slides the stretchy red fabric over her foot, and I have my answer. "Patrice said she was sorry for getting mad," she says softly, pulling the sock up to her knee. "Everything is fine."

I want to talk to her more about Patrice, but maybe now isn't the best time. I can tell that temper of hers is simmering. "Banana and I are going to the aquarium this morning and then to Miss Larkspur's for lunch," I say. "You know what is right across the street from the tea room, don't you?"

Jorgianna gives me an irritated look. Of course she knows where the Whitaker Art Gallery is.

"You want to come?" I ask.

"With you?"

"Yes, with me, who else?"

"You've never let me come with Banana and you before."

"I know, Jorgianna." I am trying not to make The Face, but she isn't helping. "I'm asking now. Come with us."

"Sorry. Can't." Both socks on, she hops off her yellow comforter and heads for her closet. "But when you go to the art gallery, be sure to see Patrice's photo."

"Patrice has a photo in the show?"

"Yeah. It's amazeballs. It's a picture of a little girl looking at a giant Pacific octopus at the aquarium."

Every hair on my neck stands at attention. "A little girl? An octopus? At the Point Defiance Aquarium?"

"Uh-huh. She's really cute. She's got pigtails and a pink coat. You have to see it, Sammi."

Something tells me I already have. My heart starts thumping against my ribs.

"It won first place in its division and second place in the show," says my sister, but between my pounding pulse and the blood rushing into my head I can barely hear her. "Patrice lost to me but she doesn't care. She still wants to be friends. How great is that?"

"Yeah. Great," I mutter. Lightheaded, I sink onto my sister's bed.

"Are we done?" Jorgianna comes out of the closet, carrying her red-and-blue plaid miniskirt and a green top with white daisies spiraling down the long sleeves. "I have to be ready by ten." She flings her clothes onto the bed next to me.

"Ready for what?"

"I'm going to the movies with my friends."

"The movies? You? The girl who refuses to go anywhere her shoes could stick to the floor is going to set foot in a theater. I don't believe it."

She lifts her chin. "I plan to keep my feet up."

If she's going out with Patrice this morning, maybe we ought to have that talk right now. "Jorgianna, I need to talk to you—"

"Isn't that what we're doing?"

"I mean, we need to have a serious discussion about middle school."

"I don't have time."

"Make time. I'm your sister."

"Big dealy woo." She gags.

My brainiac of a little sister does not say "big dealy woo." And she definitely does not gag. She is in deeper with Patrice than I thought.

"Nice attitude," I say dryly.

"I'm not trying to be a pain, Sammi. Honestly, I'm not." She smoothes out her clothes on the bed. "But I am tired of trying to make up for all the things you think are unfair between us. I can't help it if who I am isn't who you want me to be. Patrice says you have to be true to yourself and if other people don't like it, that's too bad. So this is me—being myself."

"No, this is you being a donkey butt."

She makes a *tsk, tsk* sound and flicks her finger at me like I am a bug on her arm. "Patrice says people who lash out are afraid—"

"If I hear that girl's name one more time—"

"Patrice said you'd say that."

"She did not."

Her expressions hardens. "She said my art is a reflection of you. My piece is a manifestation of how you oppress me."

I put my hands on my hips. "*She* said *that*?"

"Not exactly, but she did say you don't want me to grow into my own person. She said you'd get mad if I tried to escape from the little box you've stuffed me into."

"I'd like to stuff you into a box, all right. And ship you to Siberia."

She wags her finger at me. "Temper, Sammi."

"If you'll shut up and listen, I'll tell you—"

"Shut up and listen? Who has the attitude now? All

I've ever done is listen to you. I'm done listening. It's your turn. *You* listen to *me*." Her eyes blaze. "I'm done feeling bad about winning. I'm done feeling responsible for your happiness. From now on, I'm doing what makes *me* happy. And I told you, call me Jorgi!" With one quick motion, she rips the towel turban from her head.

I scream.

My sister's entire head is *purple*!

"You okay?" Banana pulls into a parking space in front of Miss Larkspur's Tea Room. "You hardly said a word at the aquarium."

I chip a big piece of coral polish off my thumbnail. "Sorry."

"Aren't you having a good time? Do you want to go somewhere else?"

"No. I mean, yes, I'm having a good time and no, I don't want to go anywhere else." I look out the car window at the black-and-white sign of the Whitaker Art Gallery across the street.

"Is it Jorgianna? Your mom mentioned the two of you were going through a rough patch."

"She dyed her hair purple. Not lavender. Not violet. *Purple*."

"You know your sister. She's a great blue heron soaring among mallards."

"Now she's a great purple heron—a purple heron I have to go to school with on Monday. This is all I need. I've already gotten complaints from Eden and some of my other friends over last week's flock."

"Flock?"

"Jorgianna wore a bright orange hat to school with a bunch of fake crows on it, but the birds looked real enough—I mean, dead enough—to freak out half the Wildlife Conservation Club. I had to do *a lot* of explaining to Miss Fleischmann."

She tries to hide her grin.

"Plus, we had a big fight this morning."

Her lips straighten. "I'm sorry, hon."

I drop my head into my hands and pull my bangs through my fingers.

"Most sisters go through a stage where they can't seem to do anything but fight," says Banana. "I did with mine. Ellen and your mom certainly did. When the two of them were teenagers they nearly drove me insane. Every day it seemed there was a battle, and over the silliest things, too."

"Jorgianna and I have had our battles too, but we've never been mean to each other—not like this."

Banana takes her keys out of the ignition. "Let's go inside. You'll feel better after we've had some lemon verbena tea and cucumber sandwiches. I hear they have a new molten chocolate cake. Chocolate is good for the soul, you know."

Cutting into a yummy chocolate cake with a warm, gooey center *does* sound good, but there's something I have to do first.

"Banana, could we go over to the Whitaker Gallery before we eat? I promised Jorgianna I'd see her artwork."

"Of course, sweetie."

I won the crepe flipping bet, so I don't have to visit Jorgianna's exhibit, but I want to. Plus, there's a certain photograph I *have* to see.

Inside the gallery we are met by a mousy-looking woman with a chestnut-brown Pebbles-style ponytail on the top of her head. It's thin but long, reaching almost to her waist. She is wearing a black-and-white striped suit, a frilly white blouse, and the reddest, tallest high heels I have ever seen. Banana tells her we are here to see the school district art show, and a red fingernail with dark pink tips points to an arched white hallway. "The last three galleries on the right."

"I remember," says Banana. "Jorgianna's sculpture is in the second gallery."

The moment I see my sister's art work, my breath catches. Jorgianna was right. The spotlights, the clear acrylic display stand, the little stairs that lead to the top of the cube—everything in the gallery works together to create the right atmosphere. Several overhead lights have been carefully arranged to bring out the colors of the Northwest landscape on the sides of the cube. While Banana tries to look inside the miniature Space Needle, I skip up the steps. Peering inside, I see the mound of pop cans, lightbulbs, batteries, and other trash scattered on Jorgianna's mock seashore.

"I remember when she was making this," I say to Banana, who is slowly moving the hinged blue dog's tail on the back of the box. "She was so worried." I backtrack down the steps and stand back, taking in the entire piece. "I told her everyone would love it."

FIRST PLACE, SCULPTURE.

BEST IN SHOW.

Good for you, Jorgianna, I think to myself. *Good for you.*

I know I should say it to her. I think it often, but I don't say it enough. I don't know why. I guess part of me has always felt that the more Jorgianna achieved, the less I mattered. It seemed each time she won a spelling bee or aced a test, it took a little piece away from me. It seems silly now, but that's how I felt . . .

"Exceptional, isn't it?" The woman from the reception area is back. Talk about stealth stilettos! "It's so insightful," she says. "I love the interactive feature that draws you in. This is my favorite piece in the show."

I stand tall. "It's my sister's."

She claps. "How delightful! You got here in the nick of time. The exhibit ends tomorrow. We'll be packing this piece up to send on to the state competition in Seattle."

I smile at Banana. "Wouldn't it be something if Jorgianna's artwork won the state competition?"

"If it does, it goes on to Nationals in Washington, D.C.," says the lady.

Banana whistles. "I've never been to the capital."

"Me neither," I say.

On our way out, my grandmother turns left to go back the way we came in, but I tap her arm. "Can we go to the last gallery, Banana? I mean, as long as we're here?"

I have seen every photograph in the show, so far. Patrice's entry has to be in the third gallery.

"Sure." Banana leads the way.

I am barely a few steps into the room when I see it.

My body goes numb from my brain to my ankles. Only my feet seem to be working. I let them carry me over to a square white support column where there is a photograph frame in a black mat. The image is of a girl in a pink coat staring into a large tank with a giant octopus. One of the creature's eyes looks down at her. Tentacles and fingers meet at the glass. A blue rosette with two long ribbons is attached to the artist identification card. The gold words on the rosette glisten in the light: FIRST PLACE, PHOTOGRAPHY. I glance up to read the card:

PATRICE HOUSTON

8TH GRADE, TONASKET MIDDLE SCHOOL

My breath catches. My stomach folds over. A wave of heat rises from my heart, spreading out through my shoulders and arms, then up into my neck and face. I have to clamp my lips tightly together to stifle the shriek. I am in total shock. I cannot believe it. I am staring at *my own photograph*.

"Agggggh!"

I'd held it in as long as I could. Really, I had.

Revelations

"SAMMI!" BANANA'S ARM IS AROUND ME AND I AM
slumped against her. "What's the matter?"

"I . . . I'm sorry." My mind is racing. If I tell Banana
what's going on, she'll call Mrs. Vanderslice, who'll call
Patrice's parents, who'll confront Patrice, who will lie
about the photograph. She'll say it's hers. She'll say
I'm the one who's the liar. Everyone will believe her.
Why wouldn't they? She has everyone on her side. I
can only imagine the gossip Patrice and her friends will
spread about me at school. And then there's Jorgianna.
A shiver ripples through me. How will Patrice punish

her? "I'm okay," I tell Banana. "I . . . uh . . . I almost slipped, that's all."

Gallery Lady pokes her head into the room. "Is everything all right in here?"

"Yes," says Banana. "She nearly took a tumble, but she's all right."

"Goodness!" says the woman. "Are you sure?"

"I'm okay," I say, and try to smile.

"Let's go eat," says Banana.

Before we leave, I reach out to the sapphire-blue ribbon beside my photograph. I feel one of the smooth satin tails slide through my fingers. Doesn't it just figure? I have never won anything in my life. And now that I have, no one will ever know.

While we have lunch at Miss Larkspur's Serenity Tea Room, I try to piece together what might have happened. When did Patrice get the chance to steal my photograph? And how did she do it? We don't have any classes together. I am hardly ever around her. Even at lunch I've never been closer to her than the fourth ring. I shouldn't say never. There was that one time . . .

It was a few months ago. Eden was absent from school and Patrice invited me to sit with her group. I sat in the first ring, elbow to elbow with Saturn. She almost knocked over my apple juice. Patrice was in a mood bad that day.

"Anything I can do?" I'd asked softly.

"I doubt it. I have a dumb photography assignment due in Hargrove's class. We're supposed to do a study of humanity, whatever that means."

"He's looking for photographs with emotion in them," I said. "Trust me, I know. I had Hargrove for art last semester. Hey, you want to see some of my photos? You know, for inspiration?"

"Sure."

I got out my cell phone and showed her some of my best shots: several of a wind-blown but happy Jorgianna beachcombing at Mukilteo State Park, a series of Banana on her first hang-gliding adventure, and—of course!—my new ones of a little red-headed girl in a pink coat seeing an octopus.

"These are great," said Patrice, tapping the screen. "I love this one of the octopus and the girl. I bet she is thinking, 'wow, he is so big and red,' and he's probably thinking, 'wow, she is so small and pink!'"

I chuckle. "I like to tell a story with every photograph."

"A story, huh? Good tip." Then Patrice said the nicest thing anybody had ever said to me. "You're a great photographer, Sammi."

I felt my cheeks glow. "Thanks."

"I'm going for chocolate chip cookies," said Tanith. "Anybody want to come with?"

"I will," I said, and because Patrice was still looking at my photos, I left my cell phone in her hands while I was gone.

Two minutes. That was how long it took for me to buy two chocolate chip cookies, and it was all the time Patrice needed to steal my photograph. Dumb, dumb cookies. Dumb, dumb me.

It was a big risk, stealing my picture, but knowing Patrice, she probably didn't lose much sleep over it. She figured even if I found out what she'd done I probably wouldn't make a fuss, because she was so popular and I was so . . . not. Imagine if my photo won Best in Show in the district art competition. Patrice would have ridden the glory all the way to the state level, maybe even to the nationals. But she hadn't won. She'd lost. Hooray for my little sister who never comes in second to anybody, not even the famous Saturn. ". . . gliding?"

I am jolted back to reality. "I'm sorry, what Banana?"

She sips her lemon verbena tea. "I was wondering, would you send me a couple of the photos you took of me hang gliding?"

"Okay. I've got a couple on my phone."

"You're still thinking about Jorgianna, aren't you?"

"Uh-huh." I tear a corner off the little triangular cucumber sandwich. "It isn't the fight or her purple hair. There's a lot more to it than that."

"I'm all ears."

"See, we—okay, I—I made up a contract."

She frowns. "What kind of a contract?"

"A contract that said Jorgianna and I wouldn't communicate with each other while we were both at school. It seemed like the perfect solution when my sister was skipping grades. It was supposed to be so we'd have our own lives and we wouldn't get in each other's way at school." What am I doing? I can't lie to Banana.

"Okay, it was so *she* wouldn't bug *me* at school," I say. "Except the whole thing backfired. I never should have done it."

"You can fix it. Contracts are made to be broken."

"Even among sisters?"

"Especially among sisters."

"I think it might be too late. She got in with the wrong group of friends, and now she won't listen to me. The more I try to warn her about them, the more she defends them."

Banana nods. "That's how it usually works."

"So what am I supposed to do?"

"Wait."

"*Wait?*"

"Wait and trust. Eventually, these *friends* of hers will reveal their true colors, and Jorgianna will break away from them on her own."

"How long will that take?"

"Hard to say."

That was not the answer I was hoping for. "So until she figures all of this stuff out for herself—"

"You wait."

I let out a long breath. "I wait."

I hate the idea of sitting around and doing nothing while Patrice digs her hooks deeper into Jorgianna, but I suppose my grandmother is right. What other choice do I have?

The waitress comes over. "Can I get you any dessert?"

"Chocolate molten cake!" Banana and I say at the same time.

When I slide my fork through the small mound of spongy, dark cake, a river of warm chocolate syrup flows onto the plate. Banana and I savor each luscious bite. We close our eyes. We make yummy noises. It is bliss.

Banana drops me off at home a little after three o'clock. Before heading upstairs, I check in with my parents, who are moving a rhododendron bush from one side of the yard to the other. I have no idea why. I stroll down the second-floor hallway with my head high. Jorgianna's bedroom door is open. I let only my eyes swing to the right as I slowly pass her room. I don't see anything. I take a step back. I don't hear anything. I lean over. Stick my head into her room. She's not here. Jorgianna couldn't still be at the movies, could she? It's been five hours since she left!

I go to my own room and collapse onto my bed.

Right now she's probably having the time of her life with her new besties. Who am I kidding? She's never going to give them up. How are you supposed to rescue someone who doesn't even realize she is drowning?

I bolt upright.

I'm sorry Banana, I can't do it.

I can't wait and trust. Each minute that ticks by my sister is getting closer and closer to Saturn. I can't wait for something that might never happen. I grab my phone and let my fingers fly. I tap Jorgianna's name in my contact list, and before I can come up with a million reasons why I shouldn't do it, I hit send.

Saw your art at the WAG today. Loved it. Good job! Saw Patrice's photo, too. You were right. Amaze-balls. Be sure to tell her I thought it told a great story.

Love, Sammi

A smirk curling my lips, I gently set my phone on my nightstand.

Now things ought to get interesting.

TWELVE

The Big Bang

EVERY FIVE SECONDS THERE IS A THROBBING PAIN behind my left eyeball, my stomach is boiling up some kind of witch's brew, and if I have to pretend one more time it's the funniest thing in the world when Tanith says "Forgive *meee!*" I am going to throw up this mushroom pizza with waaaay too much garlic. You'd think a place named Pizza, Pizza, Pizza would know how to make one.

At least the movie was good. Sort of. Patrice, Tanith, and India saw some boys they knew from school sitting a few rows behind us (not Noah, thank goodness). During the previews, the boys threw popcorn at us.

We, of course, had to retaliate. It was fun at first, but got annoying, especially when they hurled other stuff, like peanuts and Milk Duds. Those Duds hurt. I was secretly glad when the usher told the boys to stop or they'd have to leave. After the movie India's nanny, Vaida, offered to take us for pizza. It was nice, except for the pizza. And Tanith. That girl can talk for three and a half minutes without coming up for air.

"Who wants another slice?" asks Vaida in her Lithuanian accent. The first time Tanith and Patrice ditched us, I'd gotten to talk with her and discovered she is a college exchange student from Vilnius. "Jorgi? More pizza?"

"No, thanks. I couldn't eat another bite." My stomach is still churning. It didn't help that Patrice made us order mushrooms on the pizza, even though I said I didn't like them.

"India?" asks Vaida.

"Me too. Packed."

"Where did Patrice and Tanith go?"

"To the bathroom," says India.

Vaida puckers her lips but doesn't say the one word we are all thinking: again? "I'm going to go check on your brothers," she says to India. "When the girls get back, tell them we need to go no later than three thirty, okay?"

"Okay."

We watch Vaida head toward the play area.

"I don't think I could be an exchange student," I say. "I'd miss my family too much."

"Vaida calls and Skypes her family, but it's hard because they are, like, ten hours ahead of us in Russia."

"Actually, she's—" I stop myself.

"What?"

"She's uh . . . she's not from Russia."

"She isn't?"

"She's from Lithuania."

India twists her lips.

"It used to be part of Russia, so I could see where you might get confused," I hurry to say. "The U.S.S.R. annexed Lithuania in World War II, but when the Soviet Union fell apart in 1990, the country declared its independence. Now it's part of the European Union—sorry, I'm babbling, aren't I?"

"No, not at all."

"Has Vaida taught you anything in Lithuanian?"

"*Ačiū.*"

"Bless you," I say.

India laughs. "I didn't sneeze. I said 'Ah-chu.' It means 'thank you' in Lithuanian."

"Oh!"

"Want to hear another one?"

"Sure."

"*Viso gero.* That's good-bye."

"Vissa—?

"Gehr-oh. Vaida has this way of rolling her *R*s at the back of her throat. I'm still working on it."

"You sound good to me."

"*Ačiū,*" she says shyly. "I've been meaning to tell you how much I like your new hair color. It reminds me of pansies. You know, the dark purple ones with the bright white faces."

"*Ačiū.* I could do your hair too, if you want."

"Thanks, but if I dyed my hair my mother would kill me."

"Mine is fine with it, as long as I check with her first and use temporary dye. I got in a little bit of trouble for this. The purple came out darker than either of us expected."

"Ombré toes are about as brave as I get," India lifts her mocha-brown T-strap sandals with the turquoise beads. She wiggles a foot. Each toe is painted a different shade of pink, starting with a bright fuchsia big toe and getting lighter with each nail down the row to end at a light-pink pinkie. "I'd never have the guts to color my hair or wear some of the cool clothes you do. You're so much braver than I am. I'd die for sure if I had to move up a couple of grades and leave all my friends. That must be why Patrice likes you so much. You're fearless."

"But I'm not," I say. "Not really. I put up a good front, that's all. Tons of things scare me."

"They do? Like what?"

"You want a list?"

She leans forward, puts her elbows on the table, and rests her chin in her hands. "Uh-huh."

"Okay. Uh . . . stuff I'm scared of. Here goes. Um . . . I'm scared of choking on something in a nice restaurant and having my sister have to do the Heimlich on me in front of everybody. . . . I'm scared of big dogs that bark a lot. Same for little dogs that bark a lot. . . . Let's see, I hate those machines in the grocery store that count coins. I keep thinking they are going to start firing coins at me when I go by."

She laughs.

"Oh, and escalators," I say. "I'm always afraid I am going to get my sleeve caught in the handrail or my shoe stuck at the top and get sucked in."

India slaps the table. "Me too!"

"I won't even get on one of those things unless my sister is with me," I say.

"I wish I had a sister," she says. "I don't know Sammi that well, but she's always been nice to me. She's helped me with my homework in math. She's eaten lunch with us a few times, you know. Before, I mean . . ."

"Before everything happened with Noah."

"Yeah."

"Honestly? I don't know why Patrice got so upset over that," I say. "You guys said Noah and she were always fighting anyway. Why would you want to hang out with someone you don't even get along with?"

India hooks a lock from her brown bob behind one ear. "Patrice has her reasons. Patrice *always* has her reasons. The only reason she likes me is because I'm rich."

I stare at her in shock. "India!"

"It's true. Haven't you noticed? The only time Patrice ever talks to me is when she needs money or wants my nanny to drive us somewhere."

There is an awkward silence. I don't know what to say. I'm sure India is wrong. Patrice isn't that shallow. Is she? Suddenly, I feel prickly in my daisy shirt and plaid skirt. Our conversation was going so well and then this . . .

India cranes her neck. "Where are Tanith and Patrice, anyway? I'm giving them five more minutes, and then we're going in." She takes out her phone to check her messages. I do the same.

India hears me squeak. "What is it?"

"A message from my sister. She went to see my art-work at the gallery today. She saw Patrice's photo, too, and thought it was great. She wants me to tell her so, but I'm not sure that's a good idea. I think the farther apart I keep those two, the better."

India puts her phone in her purse. "It's sweet of

Sammi to say she liked the photo. Maybe it's her way of trying to apologize for Noah."

"Maybe," I say, putting a hand to my throbbing forehead. It's hard to think when I am in this much pain.

"Headache?"

"A little one," I say, though the truth is it feels like an angry T. rex is stomping around in my brain.

"I'm ready to go too." India gets to her feet. "This is one of the few times I get to call the shots. Let's get them."

Leading the way, India pushes on the door marked LADIES.

". . . and what is with that horrible hair col—oh, *hiiiiiii*." Tanith waves, even as her face turns a deep shade of guilt red. She is sitting on the corner of the counter. "How's it going, guys?"

Nobody answers.

Patrice stands beside Tanith. She is within an inch of the mirror, putting a layer of gloss on her lips that is almost as red as Tanith's cheeks. Patrice's eyes dart to catch my reflection for a brief second before returning to their task.

"What are you doing in here, anyway, a complete makeover?" jokes India, pretending we did not hear what we all know we heard.

"Forgive *us*," says Tanith, hopping off the granite countertop. She turns toward the mirror and fusses with her bangs.

"Better pack it up. Vaida says we are out of here in ten minutes," says India.

"We're coming," says Patrice.

India nudges me. "You should tell her."

"Later," I hiss.

Patrice slowly slides the thin red wand over her lower lip. "Tell me what?"

"It's n—nothing really," I sputter.

"If it's nothing, then you can tell me."

"She got a text from Sammi," says India. "She went to the Whitaker Gallery to see the art show."

The wand freezes. In the mirror gray-blue eyes slide to look at me.

"She said she really liked your photo," I explain. "She thought it told a great story. Those were her exact words."

A little muscle in her jaw twitches. "Mmmmm," she says, and the wand continues its slow journey across her lower lip.

I guess after what happened with Noah, Patrice is still not ready to forgive Sammi. Not that I blame her. She is still hurting. It's going to take a while.

Patrice straightens and jams the wand back into the tube of lip gloss. She smacks her lips. "Could you guys leave us alone for a sec? I need to talk to Jo Jo."

Jo Jo? Does she mean me? She must, because Tanith and India are shuffling out of the bathroom.

"We won't be long," Patrice calls after them.

"This is my fault," I blurt before the door shuts. "I wasn't going to say anything to you about the text, but India thought it could be Sammi's way of apologizing—"

"Look, Jo Jo, you know I think you're amazeballs, right?"

I dip my head.

"And I love your fierce and quirky style, I really do. It's been fun to the tenth power getting to know you."

I don't like where this is going.

"Buuuuuut . . ." Patrice's face shrivels up. ". . . I don't think we should out hang out together anymore."

I step back. "What? I know you're mad at Sammi, but—"

"It's not that. Well, it *is* that. But it's more. See, in our circle, we have to be able to trust each other. We tell secrets. We keep secrets. With you, I'd always be wondering if your sister and you were talking about me—us—behind our backs."

I can feel my temper start to simmer. "You mean the way you and Tanith were talking about me just now?"

She draws her lips in until I can't see them anymore.

"Sorry," I say.

"Jo Jo, I don't want to force you to choose sides."

"You wouldn't be. I choose you."

"But she's your sister."

"And you're my friend."

She folds her arms across her chest. "Am I?"

"Of course." How could she doubt that? She does, though. I can tell. She does. "You wouldn't be saying this if you only knew how little Sammi and I have to do with each other," I say. "We have no classes together.

We hardly see each other. We barely speak. We even have a contract so we won't get in each other's way at school, did you know that? A contract . . ." I trail off.

A frost has formed over her eyes. She has made up her mind. Patrice will not be able to get past the fact that I am connected to the person who has hurt her. She cannot trust me.

The hammering in my head now matching my heart beat for beat, I slump against the paper-towel holder. I fight back tears. I don't know how to convince her of my loyalty, so I say the only thought in my brain at this moment, the only thing I know to be true and the one thing that might possibly save me. "Patrice, you're the best friend I've ever had."

Apple-red freshly glossed lips whisper, "Sorry."

THIRTEEN

Love and Hate

BOOM!

She's home! Bouncing off my bed, I hurry down the hall. I knock on her door. "Jorgi—?" I practically bite through my tongue to keep from saying the rest of her name.

"Go away."

"Are you okay?"

"As if you care."

"What's wrong? Jorgi, what's the matter?"

I put my ear to the door, but I don't hear anything.

"Did something happen at the movies?" I call. "Do you want to talk about it?"

More silence.

Shoot! She has learned well from me.

I tap the door with my fingernails. "Did you get my text? Banana and I saw your exhibit today. You were right. I had to see it on display to really appreciate how good it is. I wanted to tell you I am so proud—"

The door flies open. "I got your stupid text," spits my sister. "Thanks for destroying my entire life."

I slap a palm to my chest. "Me? What did I do?"

"Patrice doesn't want to have anything to do with me, because you stole Noah."

"That's crazy, Jorgi. I told you, you can't steal a per—"

The door is shut in my face, nearly clipping my nose.

"—son," I finish to an empty hallway.

"What is going on?" My mom is in the doorway, her old, scrubby jeans and blue sweatshirt stained with grass and dirt.

"Jorgianna is mad at me."

"Maybe it's time to sit the two of you down—"

"No, no, Mom. That will only make it worse. I'll tell her I'm sorry when she calms down." *If* she calms down.

My mother nods, but the furrows in her forehead tell me she is not convinced Jorgianna and I can work out our differences without an intervention. I'm not sure either, but there is one good thing to come out of this: Jorgianna won't be orbiting Saturn anymore. She's been cut loose, cast adrift in the vast outer reaches of middle school space. She is lost and alone, but she is not a forgotten soul. I am here for her, if only she'd let me be.

My sister shows up to dinner with her hair back to its natural white-blond. Well, almost. It's the lightest of lavenders now. She must have shampooed it ten times to wash out all that purple. This color actually looks kind of cool. The soft shade of violet brings out her green eyes.

"I like your hair," I say gently. "And I'm sorry for what happened with Patrice."

Jorgianna does not accept my apology. Won't look at me. Won't talk to me. She pushes her tortellini around the plate a few laps, then hurries off to her room. Trudging up the stairs, I go to my room too. I have to finish my sea horse fairy tale. It's due Monday.

I can't focus on it, though. Every little sound sends me scurrying to the door to see if Jorgianna has come out of hiding. I text her. I e-mail her. I even slide a folded note under her door with a cute white kitten sticker on it. No response. At around nine, I hear her practicing her viola. At around ten, the sliver of light under her door disappears.

I am scared.

I know Jorgianna can't give me the silent treatment forever, but what if I've done permanent damage? It's all I can think about as I finish my story about Seraphina, my heroine. To save humanity from a massive tsunami, Serpahina must marry the king of the sea horses. She must become one of them. I write the climactic scene where she has to leave the family she loves, and I think about how it would crush me if I lost Jorgianna. I'd give anything to look up to find my sister hanging on my doorframe, wearing one of her bright outfits and begging to help me with my homework. I look up. She isn't there. I look down. My tears are soaking into the paper.

I go to bed, but keep waking up every two hours. I have a nightmare about trying to escape from a pack of mutant sea horses with enormous teeth. They drag me down to the bottom of the sea. As the life leaves my body, I look up into the face of Patrice.

In the morning I find the note I wrote to my sister under *my* door. On the outside, in thick red marker, she's scrawled *Return to pernicious, avaricious sender.* I don't know what either of those adjectives mean, but I have a pretty good idea, especially since the little kitten now has a pair of red-ink horns.

Real mature, Jorgianna.

Sunday is more of the same, with Jorgianna leaving a room the minute I enter it. She wants nothing to do with me. Mom takes her to her viola recital in the afternoon. For the first time ever in recital history, I am not invited. I tell myself to give it another day. Tomorrow will be better. Tomorrow Jorgianna will speak to me.

On Monday morning Mom offers both of us a ride to school.

"Is Sammi going?" asks Jorgianna, pointing her nose toward the ceiling.

"Yes, Sammi is going," I say. I am standing two feet away from her.

My sister turns away to tie her shoes. "I think I'll take the bus, Mother."

I tell myself to give it another day. Tomorrow will be better. Tomorrow Jorgianna will speak to me. In the meantime I have to go to school.

Boi-oi-oing. Boi-oi-ing. Boi-oi-ing.

Good granola. Not again!

As I walk into first period, my language arts teacher is plucking several guitar strings attached to a flat, rectangular board propped up on her desk.

"Happy Monday, sister of the full moon," she calls.

"Right back at ya, Miss Fleischmann."

I drop my backpack at my desk. "What is that thing?"

"Homemade zither," says Eden flatly.

Crumpling into my desk, I take my sea horse fairy tale out of my notebook. In a few minutes, I will turn it in to Miss Fleischmann. I do a last-minute proofread and see three round wrinkled spots on the last page. Tear stains. I hope my teacher doesn't notice them. It's too late to print out another copy. I hope Miss Fleischmann likes my fairy tale, but she probably won't. I'll get another blah B. I am queen of the Bs. Queen B. I giggle to myself.

"Was it something I said?" I turn to see a grinning Charlie.

"Hey, Charlie."

He stops folding a silver gum wrapper. "Gum?"

"Sure." I take a stick. "Thanks."

Charlie goes back to his origami.

Eden turns to sit sideways in her seat. "I've been thinking. From now on, we should sit at a table next to the windows at lunch. It's closer to the deli and the light is much better there. Agree?"

I know what she is doing and I love her for it.

"Are you sure?" I ask. "If you waited by yourself at our table, I bet Patrice would invite you—"

"I don't want to go without you. It wouldn't be any fun. Besides, I'm tired of waiting. I'd rather just live and be happy. Know what I mean?"

I do.

Once the concert ends and roll is taken, Miss Fleischmann says, "Hand in your fairy tales, please. Pass them forward to the front of your row."

The inside of my mouth morphs into the Sahara Desert. This is it.

Charlie takes Lorzeno's paper, puts his assignment on top, and hands them to me. I put my story on top of Charlie's and give the pile to Eden.

A minute later Charlie is tapping my shoulder. "Hold out your hand."

I do, thinking he is going to give me a stick of gum. Instead, Charlie drops a silver piece of paper into my palm. It's one of his origami gum wrappers. I look closer. It's a sea horse! I study its long, scooping snout and tiny, curled tail. He's even put teeny folds in the body to give the sea horse ridges. It's a perfect replica!

"A little something for luck," he says.

I smile. "Thanks, Charlie."

I place the little silver sea horse at the corner of my desk. When it comes to winning over Miss Fleischmann, I'll take all the luck I can get.

"Do you want to come to my baseball game on Saturday?" Noah asks. We are walking to the public library after school.

"Okay."

"My dad could pick you up on the way."

"Okay."

"Or we could take you, and your parents could pick you up," he says.

"Okay."

"Or you could have one of your parents drop you off, and we could bring you home."

"Okay."

He stops. "Sammi, you don't have to come if you don't want to."

"I do, Noah. I'm sorry if it seems like I'm not paying attention. It's just that—"

"What? You don't like me anymore?"

"No! I lov—I mean, I like you." I slap a hand over my mouth. I can't believe I almost said "love." Slowly, I take my hand away, unsure if I can trust myself. "Of course I like you. I was thinking about something else."

"What?"

"You'll laugh."

"Try me."

"I was thinking about . . . french fries. I didn't get lunch today."

Noah laughs.

I point at him. "See?"

"Come on," he says, reaching for my hand.

There was a good reason why I didn't eat today. First, Eden and I had to break free from Saturn's orbit, and it took a little longer than we thought. We had to try out a couple of tables until we found one we liked. After that I bought a Cobb salad that I had every intention of eating, but each time somebody came into the cafeteria, I'd pop up to see if it was Jorgianna. I did it so much Eden started calling me a Sammi-in-the-box. Then I sent Eden to check the bathroom nearest to the cafeteria to be sure Jorgianna wasn't inside sobbing her eyes out. She wasn't. I know she didn't take her lunch this morning, so what did my sister eat? And more important, where did she eat it?

Noah and I stop at Hot Diggity's for an order of fries and two chocolate milks to go. As we cross the street toward the library park, Noah reads my mind. "You want to eat in the gazebo?"

"Sure."

The last time Noah and I were here together, the park was packed with hundreds of people searching for books at the big library book sale. Now we are by ourselves, except for the people going into and coming out of the library. As we walk down the gravel path, the breeze kicks up. The wind plucks pink cherry blossoms off the trees to create a petal ballet. I cannot help but think of this place as ours. I wonder if Noah thinks of it that way too.

There is a bench on each wall of the hexagonal-shaped gazebo. We choose the one that faces the ornamental cherry trees. Noah hands me a bottle of chocolate milk. He takes the box of crinkle fries out of the bag and sets it on the rail behind us. As steam rises off the fries, my stomach gurgles.

I shake my milk, open it, and take a drink. The thick sweetness of cold chocolate slides down my throat, through my chest, and into my hollow stomach. I sigh. "I love chocolate milk." Noah doesn't answer. I look over at him. His milk is half gone already.

Noah wipes a hand across his mouth. "Me too."

I want to ask him about Patrice, but I can't. Does he still like her? I want to ask him how he feels about me, but I'm not brave enough to do that, either.

"I'll be a little late to the dance Friday night," says Noah. "I have baseball practice."

"Okay." I place my milk at my feet.

"Also, I should warn you, I'm not a very good dancer."

"Me neither."

"I'm better at line dancing." Noah clicks his heels twice, taps each toe on the floor, crosses then uncrosses his ankles, and ends with kicks out to the side with each foot.

"That's good. Show me how to do that." He goes through the routine again, this time more slowly so I can copy him. I do everything exactly as he does it, except I get a little enthusiastic with the kick and my right foot hits my chocolate milk, sending it onto its side. It pours out onto the wood. "Oh no!"

Before I can move, a long arm shoots out over my knees to rescue the bottle. Noah straightens. I hold out my hand, expecting him to give back my chocolate milk, but he doesn't. He doesn't say or do anything. I look up. Sage-green eyes are as close as they have ever been to me. And coming closer. Lips touch mine quickly, and lightly, like fairy wings. I taste chocolate. I shiver in my moss sweater, even though the tree limbs, heavy with cherry blossoms, haven't moved since we sat down. Everything around me goes still and silent, and I am certain time has stopped. Noah lifts his head and we smile at each other. My brain goes blank. I forget about Jorgianna and Patrice. I forget about Miss Fleischmann and my A. I even forget I am hungry.

Noah and I turn so we are sitting side by side on the bench. A strange sensation begins to spread through me. It starts in my heart and flows outward, like an electrical current. It zings up to the top of my skull, then out to my fingernails and down through the tips of my toes. Here and now, everything that is wrong in my life is suddenly and mysteriously eclipsed by this one right. As usual, Banana was dead-on.

Chocolate *is* good for the soul.

So is love.

FOURTEEN

Inside Out and Upside Down

IN FIRST-PERIOD SCIENCE I GET A 100 PERCENT PLUS earn all the bonus points on Wannamaker's chemical reactions test. I am told it's happened only twice in his eighteen years of teaching. In second-period history I get an A-plus on my paper on Clara Barton, the Civil War nurse who founded the American Red Cross. She has always been one of my heroes. I always wanted to be a nurse, but my mother has always wanted me to be a doctor. In third-period math Mr. Withey, the substitute, struggles with calculating permutations. I step in to show the class how to solve one of our story problems and end up finishing the lesson for him. I give no homework. The class applauds.

Everything is going perfectly in my new school. And I am miserable.

I have been steering clear of the cafeteria all week so I don't run into Patrice and her friends or, for that matter, Sammi. I don't mind eating alone, but I don't want my sister feeling sorry for me. I'm still not speaking to Sammi. I know I am being mean, but I want her to feel, if only for a little while, the way I feel all the time. Isolated. Frustrated. Helpless.

After third period I do what I have been doing for the past five days. I get my lunch from the vending machines in the atrium. Today's menu: spicy chipotle chips, corn nuts, butterscotch pudding, orange juice, and a two-pack of s'mores-flavored Pop-Tarts. My mother would have a heart attack if she knew what I was eating for lunch. I wish they sold Tums, too, for the stomachache that always kicks in during fifth-period PE.

I take my lunch outside to the courtyard. It's sunny, though chilly, for late April. Most of the kids sitting in the courtyard are in groups of two to four, though a couple of them are alone—a girl and a boy. The girl is reading, absently plugging grapes into her mouth. The boy's head of blond hair is bent so far over his tablet, I can't see his face. I don't go up to either of them. Instead, I follow the main circular path and turn right at the overgrown holly bushes before I reach the other side of the courtyard. The offshoot leads to a dead end with a small iron bench. It's hidden, yet gets a sliver of sun during lunchtime.

"Look, Patrice." I lift my pudding in the air. "I'm starting with dessert. Oh, the horror!" I happily yank off the top. At least I don't have to worry about someone telling me what to eat and when to (or when not to) eat it. Goose bumps go up my arms as I remember her sharp warning. "No tacos, Jorgianna. Never tacos!" Next Monday I am buying a taco. I will eat it alone, but I will get one.

I have decided to stop fighting fate. It's time I accept that I am destined to go through life without a single friend, a close sibling, or, apparently, a locker. Miss Dunham in the office said my locker assignment wasn't a typo. Since she was new, she'd gotten out the big map and given me directions to find it. I followed her map to the letter and ended up in D wing by the orchestra room. Unfortunately, all of the locker numbers were in the six hundreds. After going down a dark staircase with only a bare, flickering lightbulb and a wolf spider the size of Idaho to guide me, I decided a rectangular metal storage bin wasn't worth risking my life. Unless this school gets some kind of locker GPS, I'll be toting everything I own around on my back for the rest of the semester.

Snapping off a corner of my Pop-Tart, I crumble and toss it to the chickadees skittering at my feet. A big crumb accidentally bounces off a tiny feathered head. "Sorry," I say as he picks up the tidbit with his beak.

I lift my face to a beam of sun edging into my secret garden and take a deep breath. It's nice not having to worry, *Am I saying the right thing at the wrong time?* Or the wrong thing at the right time? Or the wrong thing at the wrong time? Or anything that anyone in this group even wants to hear? "Did you hear that Tanith?" I say out loud. "Four questions in a row!"

". . . you're coming to the dance, right?"

"Abso-positively."

A couple of girls are coming around the main loop. I scoot to the farthest corner of my bench. I lean back so I am well hidden. Unfortunately, there's a holly bush right behind me. Ouch!

"I hope Charlie comes."

"Noah, too. I have a crush on him."

"He likes Sammi Tremayne, you know."

"I know. She's so lucky."

"Jealous?"

"Who wouldn't be? I'm just glad he isn't hanging out with Patrice anymore. That girl is so mean. She cheated off me in history—"

"Careful, Bree. The forest could be full of gossiping fairies."

"Right."

They pass my turnoff.

I slide forward. I don't see any blood seeping through my sweater, but then, it *is* red. I look at my Pop-Tart, flattened in my rush to get out of sight. What has happened to me? Elementary school had its haters, for sure, but I never let them change me. Now I'm hiding in the bushes, talking to myself, and the only friends I have are ones that chirp.

Not so long ago I was a great blue heron soaring among mallards.

These days, I am a bunny.

A tiny, terrified, junk food–eating bunny.

"You don't look so good." Hanna Welch's face hovers in front of mine.

"Must be too many sit-ups right after lunch." We are getting dressed after PE. Hanna usually dresses on the other side of the locker room, so for her to come all this way I really must look sick. "I forgot it was a fitness test day," I say.

"My cousin Carolyn has an ulcer. Can you imagine having an ulcer at thirteen?"

Yes. Yes, I can, but of course I say, "No, that's awful." I put my head through my red turtleneck sweater with the two big yellow patch pockets in front. I pull the sweater down and straighten the pockets so they line up with the two hip pleats on my sapphire-blue miniskirt.

"Wickedly great outfit," says Hanna.

"Yeah, if you don't mind looking like a big Lego," snorts Tanith. She is standing at a locker behind us, buttoning a pink blouse.

"I happen to like Legos," Hanna says.

I sit on the bench to put on my boots, and a tidal wave of acid rolls through my stomach. It splashes up into my throat and I have to swallow quickly to keep from throwing up. I taste spicy chipotle chips and butterscotch.

Hanna is beside me. "You really look sick. Do you want to go to the nurse's office?"

"I'll be okay. I just need a minute."

"I'll get you some water." Hanna pops up and comes back with a paper cup of water from the cooler. "Sip this."

When I finish the water, I reach into my locker for one of my boots. My stomach sloshes, but the sour, rolling sensation from a few minutes ago is gone. Hanna hands me the other boot. I zip them both and sit up. "See? Perfectly perfect."

"Stay there." Hanna stands. "I'm getting my coat and backpack and then I'm walking you to sixth period. Cross your heart you won't move a muscle until I get back."

Crossing my heart, I can't help my grin. She sounds like Sammi. I miss my sister telling me what to do. It's the sort of thing that little sisters pretend we don't like, but secretly we do. Hanna is back in less than two minutes. She won't let me carry my backpack. Once we are outside the gym, I take a few deep breaths of fresh air. "I feel a lot better."

"You look a lot better," says Hanna. "You had me scared for a minute. Your face went so green I thought you were going to turn into a four-leaf clover."

"No chance of that."

"Where are we going, anyway?"

"A wing. Language arts. Miss Fleischmann."

"Geez, Jorgianna, what do you have in here—cement?" Hanna staggers. She is carrying my pack on her right shoulder and her own pack on her left.

"I can take that now," I say.

"It's okay. I've got it. Are you into weight lifting?"

"I . . . um . . . sort of carry all of my stuff around because . . . well, the truth is, I can't find my locker." There. I said it. I rush on when I see her stunned reaction. "I know, I know, you were going to show me on my first day and then Patrice came along and off I went with her. I'm sorry. I should have stayed with you. Patrice and her friends had no idea where my locker was. So then I went back to the office and asked Mrs. Dunham, and she gave me directions but I think her compass was way off, because I ended up in the basement."

Hanna shakes her head. "Even though you did ditch me for Patrice, I still would have shown you where your locker was, Jorgianna. All you had to do was ask."

"You know where it is?"

"Uh-huh."

"You're positive?"

"Of course. Everyone in the NSWC goes through training—that's the New Student Welcome Club. We know where everything is, including the nicest bathrooms, the best vending machines, and every single locker. I'll show you where yours is after school, unless you have a bus to catch." She snaps her fingers. "I know—I could show you at the dance tonight."

"Let's meet after school." I run a hand through my violet hair. "I'm not . . . not going to the dance."

Although I do not share them with Hanna, I have four reasons for not going to the dance.

Reason #1: My contract with Sammi.

Reason #2: Patrice and her friends.

Reason #3: After my last experience trying to make friends, I am not in any hurry to repeat the process.

Reason #4: I have never been to a middle school dance. I have no idea what to do and I can't ask my sister for advice.

We are at Miss Fleischmann's room. Hanna hands over my backpack. "You're sure you're okay?" When I nod, she says, "I'll meet you here after class and we'll get you to your locker."

"Thanks, Hanna."

Sixth period cannot go fast enough. As promised, Hanna appears a few minutes after the final bell. "Come with me," she says, raising her eyebrows mysteriously as she walks backward down the hall. Hanna takes me to the end of A wing. We turn left and head through B and C wing, as Mrs. Dunham had instructed me. We end up near the orchestra room in front of a group of ten lockers.

My heart sinks. I have been here before. "Hanna, these are the 600s. See? 601, 602, 603 . . ." I walk down the line. "Mine is 904, remember? We're in the wrong place."

"No, we're not. You, Jorgianna Tremayne, are the proud owner of an upside-down locker."

They look right-side up to me. "Am I going to have to stand on my head to open it or something?"

"No." She laughs. "See, over the years, the numbered stickers on a lot of the lockers started falling off and everybody kept putting them back on. At some point, somebody put their nine on upside down as a joke, and everyone else in the row started doing the same thing. When the janitors finally got around to painting the numbers on the lockers, no one told the painter, and he painted sixes instead of nines. Every year Mr. Ostrum says he's going to have them repainted, but we think they are cool, so we keep talking him out of it. It's tradition now. This one"—she points to 604—"is really 904. This is yours."

"So Mrs. Dunham *did* send me to the right place, after all."

"She's only been here for a month, so I bet she hasn't heard the story yet."

"But most everybody else at TMS knows."

"Of course. It's legend."

"Pa—I mean, nobody told me."

"I'm not surprised." A shadow crosses her face. "*Some* people won't tell the new students about them. They love watching somebody run all over the place trying to find their locker. They think it's hilarious. I don't. Not one bit. And I'm not afraid to say so to *certain* people either."

She knows that I know she's talking about Patrice, but neither of us want to say her name out loud.

"I'm with you," I say.

She tips her head. "I am kind of surprised Sammi didn't clue you in when you told her you were having trouble finding your locker."

"I never told her," I confess. "I wanted to do this one all by myself."

"I hear you." She rolls her eyes. "I have three sisters."

"Three! How do you do it? I have enough trouble with one." I dig out my locker card. Hanna stands over my shoulder, instructing me on how to clear the dial and enter the combination. I lift the handle and the door opens. It's empty. "It's a miracle!"

"You're lucky, you know. These lockers are popular. A lot of kids want them."

I start unloading my backpack. It's such a relief! I

cannot wait to have a normal load of books to carry again. My sore back and shoulders will be happy too.

"Hi, girls!"

I stop stuffing books into my locker to wave at the lady click-clacking her way toward us in a lemonade-colored suit and matching low-heeled pumps.

"Hi, Mrs. Vanderslice," we say.

The superintendent's fluffy bouffant hairdo, a.k.a. the Leaning Tower of Vanderslice, is at about a seventy-degree angle today. Near the top a little canary on a clip bounces as if trying to build a nest in the massive column of fluff.

Mrs. Vanderslice puts a hand on my shoulder. "And how are we settling into middle school life, dear?"

"We—I mean, *I'm* doing fine."

"Lovely, lovely. I'm on my way to a meeting, but let's chat at the dance tonight."

"D . . . dance?" I gulp.

"I'm one of the chaperones. You are coming, aren't you, Jorgianna?"

"I don't know, Mrs. V. I have so much homework—"

Two of her three chins wobble in disapproval. "Homework can wait. We moved you ahead in your studies, Jorgianna, with the understanding that you would not neglect your emotional growth."

"But I—"

"Social activities are an important part of middle school life."

"I know but—"

"I'd be happy to discuss the matter with your parents, if you'd like."

"No, Mrs. Vanderslice. You don't have to do that. I'll go to the dance."

"Excellent." Mrs. Vanderslice continues on her way. As she click-clacks down the hall, she tosses over her shoulder, "Remember, Jorgianna, as Mark Twain once said, 'There's more to life than simply increasing its speed.'"

"Um . . . actually, I'm pretty sure it was Gandhi . . ."

There is no point in finishing. The superintendent is already click-clacking up the stairs.

I turn to Hanna.

She wears a satisfied smile. "Want a ride?"

FIFTEEN

Trapped in Paradise

JORGIANNA STARES OUT THE WINDOW ON HER SIDE of the car. I do the same on my side. We are only a few feet apart, but it feels like miles. Jorgianna crosses her legs. I watch the pointed toe of her black boot swing back and forth. She's paired her stretchy black knee-boots with a red eyelet skirt. A red camisole peeks through her white lace tunic. Ten or twelve strings of white pearls hang to her waist—probably about eight strands more than I'd wear, but for her it's tame. I want to tell her she looks good, but I'm afraid I might set her off. Jorgianna would probably insist I call her JT and make Dad turn the car around so she could go home and dye her hair green. I figured it's best to keep quiet, but I wonder, is she *ever* going to talk to me?

Dad makes a left into the middle school parking lot. Instead of heading for the drop-off curb, he pulls into a space in the last row of parking spots.

Thank you, Dad!

He turns in his seat. "I'll be in this spot in two hours, girls, unless you call me to come sooner, okay?"

We nod.

"Your mom gave you money, right?"

We nod again.

"Have fun, Sunbeam and Moonbeam. Don't break too many hearts."

Jorgianna and I snort.

My sister motions with her hand, waving me to go on ahead of her.

I push up the sleeves of my sky-blue blazer with the little purple forget-me-nots and get out of the car. I start across the parking lot. It's weird to be at school when the sun is going down, rather than coming up. I walk with the hope that if I go slowly enough, Jorgianna will catch up to me. My new jeans are doing a *swish-*

swishing thing with each step. Maybe I shouldn't have worn them. I don't want to seem like I am trying too hard.

Inside the foyer a hand-painted banner reads WELCOME TO PARADISE. The sign is trimmed with a garland of silk orchids in a rainbow of colors. On each side of the entrance to the cafeteria, an inflatable palm tree sways. Overhead, the fringe of a thatched roof made out of plastic flutters each time someone opens an outside door. Mrs. Delpy, Stella, Bridget, and a few other students are at a table next to one of the palm trees, selling tickets.

"Sammi!" Eden hurries over and we get in line behind a group of seventh grade girls. "Love your new jeans."

She always knows exactly what to say to make me feel better.

"How do I look?" She twirls in a pink-and-white floral sundress and white sandals. Eden always dresses to theme. She has tucked a white silk gardenia behind her ear.

"Stunning, as always." I peek over her shoulder

to see if Jorgianna has made it inside yet. I don't see her, but I know she's here. My sister has gotten good at keeping out of sight.

"Where's Noah?" asks Eden.

"He's got baseball practice, so he's going to be late. He said he'd text me if it was more than a half hour— oh, shoot!" I slap my hands against my blazer pockets. "I left my phone in the car."

"We should Velcro the thing to you. Then you'd never forget it."

"I'll bet Jorgianna could make me a stylish phone hat."

Eden giggles. "With birds on it too."

I pay for my ticket and make a fist for Stella Nguyen to stamp. When she takes the stamp away, I stare at the brown-ball imprint on the top of my hand.

"It's supposed to be a coconut," says Stella.

"Ohhh."

Bridget looks at my white tee and blue blazer and lifts a pale-blue lei out of her box. "Aloha," she says, placing the flowers around my neck.

"Cute," I say, fingering the silk petals.

"It was Patrice's idea."

I let out a skeptical grunt. Bridget tips her head, and I tap my chest and cough, as if I had to clear my throat all along.

Eden gets a pink lei to match her dress, and we stroll under the plastic thatched roof into the darkened cafeteria. A few steps inside, we pause and wait for our eyes to adjust. It's about ten degrees warmer in here and smells like popcorn and cookie dough. The piercing bass reverberates up through my feet, threatening to derail my heartbeat.

Boom, boom, ba-boom, boom. Boom, boom, ba-boom, boom.

Beams of red, blue, and green light circle the dance floor in time to the beat. The tables have been pushed back against the wall, and although there is plenty of room to dance, only a few people are out there. This is typical for the first half hour.

Eden points to the back of the room, where they are selling snacks. "Do you want anything?" she yells over the pounding music.

I shake my head. "OMG, is that Mrs. Vanderslice?"

The superintendent is busting some moves, trying to get the kids sitting on the tables to get up and dance. She does the gunslinger, pointing at the air in time to the beat, her yellow hips pitching from side to side.

"Whoa!" Eden squeals. "I cannot unsee that."

Laughing, we turn away.

Eden and I run out onto the dance floor. It's how we always dance—doing our own thing side by side—until we get the courage to ask a boy to dance, or vice-versa, or a slow song comes on and we take a break. I have a billion times more courage at dances than I do at school. Maybe it is because it is dark. Or because the music is loud. Or because even the popular boys, the ones who don't want to talk to you at school, will dance with you if you are brave enough to ask. At my first school dance it took me exactly one hour and forty-nine minutes to get up the nerve to ask Corey Bateman to dance. He said yes. We danced the last dance, "Stairway to Heaven." And was it ever.

A few songs later I see Jorgianna. She is sitting by herself on one of the tables next to some coats. Knees pulled up, she is hunched over her phone. I bet she is playing chess. I can relate. Games were my go-to strategy for my first few dances last year until I figured out all the people you think are watching you aren't really watching you at all. I try to get Jorgianna's attention, but she is two inches from her screen. Eden and I dance past her. The next time I see my sister, about fifteen minutes later, I am dancing a slow dance with Charlie. Jorgianna is in the same spot on the same table, still nose to screen. Is she going to sit there all night?

"Come on, Jorgianna, ask someone to dance," I murmur.

"Sorry." Charlie pulls back. "Did I step on your toes?"

I look down at him. "No. It's me—well, my sister, actually. It's her first dance. I don't think she's having much fun."

"First dances can be rough."

I nod toward her table as we go by. "Look at her, over there all by herself. Like a dead bug."

"That's your sister, huh?" He gives a wry grin. "It'll get better."

"I hope so. It couldn't get much worse."

When the song ends, Eden appears. She points to the back of the room, which is our signal for "let's take a break." We head to the snack bar and get two 7-Ups. Still trying to catch my breath, I pop open my can of soda.

"Hi, Sammi." It's Cara.

"Hi."

She won't look at me. She keeps licking her lips.

"Thirsty?" I offer her my 7-Up.

Cara shakes her head and licks her lips again. "I . . . uh . . . Patrice sent me."

The music is starting again. "What?" I ask.

"Patrice," she says louder. "She wants to talk to you."

"Me?" I tap my chest. "Now?"

"Uh-huh."

"What does she want?" demands Eden.

"I don't know. Honestly, I don't. She'll meet you in the bathroom. Also . . . um . . . she said to come alone." Cara scuttles away before Eden and I can quiz her further.

Eden glues herself to my arm. "Don't go."

"Why not? I'm not under her spell anymore."

"That's why you shouldn't go."

I hand her my soda. "It'll be okay. I won't be long."

"Text me if you get in trouble."

I lift my hands to remind her: no phone.

She groans. "I'm giving you exactly ten minutes and then I'm coming in." As I go, Eden adds, "And I'm bringing Mrs. Vanderslice with me."

I know my best friend. She is not kidding.

It's a big contrast, going from the flashing lights and thundering music to the dull fluorescent lights and stillness of the hallway. I hurry down to the girls' bathroom at the end of the hall. As I go in, I meet Bridget and Stella coming out.

"Hi," I say.

"Hi," they mutter, their eyes down.

Patrice is at the long mirror, putting on mascara. Tanith is waving her nails under the hand dryer.

I look at Patrice's reflection. "If I have to be alone, then so do you. It's only fair."

"You can't tell me what to do," says Tanith.

"Go, Tanith," orders Patrice.

Tanith grumbles and gives me a dirty look, but she follows orders.

I lean back, checking the stalls for feet. I don't see any. We are alone.

I'm super nervous. I have to pee.

Not now, I tell myself. *Now you need to be strong, and the strong hold their pee. Be confident. Be courageous. Most of all, be quick.*

"Is this about my photo?" I ask. "The one you stole

from my phone and entered in the district art competition as your own?"

Turning from the mirror, Patrice puts a hand to her heart. "Sammi, I am so sorry about that. I only borrowed it for my photo assignment. I didn't know—"

"Borrowed?"

"Well, you weren't using it. It didn't seem like any big dealy woo. Nobody was supposed to know."

Nobody was supposed to know. Is she kidding me?

"I didn't give you permission to use the picture for an assignment," I say. "And I definitely didn't say it was okay for you to enter it in the art contest."

"That wasn't my fault," she barks, pointing her mascara wand at me. "I didn't find out about the contest until *after* Mr. Hargrove had entered my—your—photo in it. And then I was stuck. I couldn't tell him the truth. It was too late."

"It's never too late to tell the truth. *You* won a blue ribbon with *my* photo, Patrice. That's wrong."

Taking a step toward me, she sniffles like she is about to cry. "I said I was sorry. You aren't going to tell, are you?"

"I don't know." I am pretty sure I'm not going to

turn Patrice in, but I don't want her to know that.

There's something moving on the floor behind her. Is that a foot in the last stall? It is! I see a dark brown sandal with turquoise beads and five toes, each painted a different color of pink. The foot slowly slips back and out of sight.

"I have an idea," says Patrice. "I think I know a way we can work it out so we're all happy."

I eye her. What's to work out? She stole my photo. End of story. "What do you mean?"

"I was thinking, it must be so hard on Jo right now," says Patrice.

Jo? I stiffen. I'm guessing she means my sister, but what does Jorgianna have to do with this?

"She must hate being caught between us," says Patrice. "She eats lunch by herself in the atrium. Vending machine food. Did you know that?"

I didn't, but I lift my chin and say, "Yes."

"She has no friends at all. Poor thing. She's been sitting out there in the same spot all night." Patrice pouts. "Nobody is talking to her or dancing with her. She looks so sad."

I grit my teeth. I don't need her to tell me anything

about my sister. "Jorgianna will be fine. She needs to make some *new* friends."

"It's not that easy," she says. "Especially at our school."

Is she trying to tell me she is keeping other girls from being friends with Jorgianna? Patrice has a lot of power. Just ask Hanna and Lauren.

"Anyway," Patrice says, "I thought, if you were to keep quiet about the photo, I could—I mean, we could—make up with Jo. We could be friends again."

Oh-oh-oh! Now I get it. Patrice wants to make a deal. She wants to be absolutely, positively sure I keep my mouth shut about her stealing my photograph, and she's using my sister's happiness to do it.

"You know it's what Jo wants," says Patrice. "She wants to be back with us, and we want her back too. It's the best thing for everybody, Sammi. It's the perfect solution."

My mouth drops open. I can't believe this girl. Worse, I can't believe Eden and I wasted eight whole months trying to inch our way into Saturn's inner ring. What were we thinking?

Patrice is right about one thing, though. Jorgianna

is alone. And my sister blames me for it. Patrice is giving me a chance to fix things. If I agree, Jorgianna gets her friends back. If I don't, I doom my sister to be a middle school outcast.

Patrice tosses her mascara into her purse. "Oh, and there's one other thing I'm going to need for you to do, Sammi."

"What?"

Glacial gray-blue eyes drill through mine. "Stay away from Noah."

SIXTEEN

First Dance

"WANNA DANCE?"

I am sitting on one of the tables, playing a game of chess on my phone. I have a wall on one side of me and a pile of coats on the other side, and still I say to him, "You mean me?"

"Yep." His overgrown blond hair bounces into his eyes.

"No, thanks."

"Come on. This is a good song."

"I like the song all right. I'm a terrible dancer."

"You can't be that bad."

"I am the worst."

"The worst, huh?"

"Without a doubt." I go back to my chess game. Instead of leaving, he kneels on one of the seats in front of me. "Tell you what—if I can find three people who dance worse than you, will you dance then?"

"O . . . okay, I guess so."

"I'm Charlie, by the way."

I touch the neck of my lace tunic. "Jorgianna."

He rubs his chin. "All right, let's see what we have here."

While Charlie searches the crowd for horrible dancers, I play another game of level-nine chess on my phone. I win in twelve moves.

"Is this yours?" Charlie points to the small gold purse on the seat next him.

"Yes."

"It's buzzing."

I reach for it. "It's my sister's phone. She's always forgetting it." I unzip my bag and take out Sammi's cell phone. I want to give it to her, but I'd be breaking our contract. I touch the screen. It's a text from Banana. I start to put the phone away, then think, *What if it's an emergency?* I'd better read it. I open the message.

Hi S, don't forget to send me your photos. Love, Banana

There!" Charlie is pointing to a tall dark-haired boy who is dancing like a giraffe stuck in the mud. He *is* awful. Reluctantly, I hold up my index finger.

I text Banana back:

I'm at the school dance. Which photos?

I give thumbs-down to Charlie's next two finds, a girl doing a Beyoncé-style strut and a boy shaking like he has a nest of wasps in his pants.

"What do you mean?" He throws his arms out.

"Those two are awful."

"I'm the judge and I say they are still better than me. Keep looking."

"You're not going to make this easy, are you?"

Smart boy.

Another text from Banana comes in.

The ones of me hang gliding, remember? No rush. Send them tomorrow. Have fun tonight. I hope you are dancing with that cute boy from the book sale. Love, B

I have nothing else to do. I might as well look for the photos Banana wants. Tapping on Sammi's photo gallery, I start scrolling through her pictures. I see a series of shots Sammi took of me at the beach last fall. The wind is blowing my hair straight up and I am laughing as I skip from rock to rock. These are followed by a set of pics at the aquarium. No surprise there. Sammi loves the Point Defiance Aquarium. I slide through pictures of sea horses, otters, dolphins, various fish tanks—ooh! A giant Pacific octopus. I tap it so it comes up full screen. A little girl in a pink coat is clamped to the exhibit window as she watches an octopus watching her. I've seen this photo before. It's Patrice's entry in the art show. Sammi must have taken a picture of it when she went to the gallery with Banana last week.

"Got one!" Charlie points to a kid patting his head, jutting out his neck, twisting his hips, and doing some kind of soccer kick with his feet.

Is he dancing or having a seizure? Dancing. Definitely dancing.

Charlie's got me. I hold up two fingers.

Charlie pumps his fist. "Two down, one to go."

I look at the photo on my sister's phone again. Something isn't right. There's no black mat around the picture or white wall behind it. This isn't a photo of a photo. Plus, from all the pictures that come before and after this one, it's obvious my sister *is* at the aquarium. There's no doubt this is *Sammi's* photo. The hairs on the back of my neck stand at attention. If that's true, then—

Charlie is tapping on my shin. "There!"

"Where? I don't see anybody."

"The lady by the door."

"You mean Mrs. Vanderslice?"

Mrs. V is flapping her plump arms while doing some sort of toe-heel, toe-heel step out to each side. She looks like a yellow hen about to lay an egg.

"Disqualified," I say. "She's an adult."

"We didn't say anything about age. She only has to be worse than you."

He's right. Watching the Leaning Tower of Vanderslice do her pendulum thrash, I cannot deny it. Mrs. V *is* worse than me. I have no choice. I must give Charlie three fingers. And I must dance.

Putting both phones in my purse, I sling the strap over my head. The moment I climb off the table, the music ends. I'm saved! I am about to sit down again when the DJ announces, "All right, kids, we're going slow things down for this next one, and it's ladies choice. So choose your lads wisely, lovely ladies, or the toes you lose could be your own."

Charlie is standing. He is waiting for me to choose him.

I shake my head vigorously as the speakers crackle with the first few notes of Elton John's "Can You Feel the Love Tonight." "I . . . I can't slow dance."

"For a girl who has the guts to skip a couple of grades, you sure say 'can't' a lot."

Charlie knows who I am! He also has a point.

"Can you rock back and forth?" he asks.

I nod.

"Then you can slow dance." He takes my hand and pulls me onto the dance floor before I can come up with a decent argument.

Facing Charlie, I regret not putting on a second layer of deodorant. I have never even held a boy's hand before, and now I am going to dance with one! I feel like I am about to take a test I didn't study for. I haven't had that feeling since kindergarten.

Charlie puts his hands on my waist. I hope he can't feel the butterflies in my stomach, because there's a whole monarch migration going on in there. I watch the couple behind Charlie and place my frozen hands at the top of his shoulder the way I see the girl do with her partner. Charlie's neck is warm. Turning my head, I watch the feet of another girl next to me. She's swaying back and forth, hardly moving at all. I copy her. I try not to lock my knees. I don't want to tip over. I try not to breathe too much. Or too little. Charlie leads us, and we make a path in the shape of a small trapezoid. As the music plays, the monarch stomach butterflies start to land. I dare to close my eyes. But not for long—not for more than thirteen seconds at a time. I don't want to crush his feet.

"You're doing fine," Charlie says into my ear.

The music has stopped. Is the song over? Already?

Charlie lets me go. He steps back. "Not so bad, huh?"

"Not so bad."

He gives a small salute, and we go in opposite directions. I try not to skip back to my table, but there may be a slight springiness in my feet. Yippee! I did it. My first dance at my first dance. I can't wait to tell Sammi.

Sammi!

I was having so much fun I almost forgot. Yanking the zipper of my purse, I grab Sammi's phone and tap the screen. I go to the gallery and find the photo of the little girl at the aquarium. I start scanning the dance floor for my sister, but then remember I can't talk to her. We're on school grounds. And we still have a contract. Dang! There is one other option. I could ask someone else—someone who used to be my friend. But will she even talk to me? And will she tell the truth? There is only one way to find out.

Patrice and her friends are camped in the opposite corner of the cafeteria. I've been trying not to look their way all night. Now I lift myself to my full height, fill my lungs, and march over to them. Their seating order on the table is pretty much the same as it is at lunch, with Tanith perched on one side of Patrice, and Mercy and Cara on the other side. India sits next to Tanith. She stares at her brown T-strap sandals with the turquoise beads and curls her ombré pink toes under.

"Look who's here," snickers Tanith, inspecting me

from pearls to boots. "Selling jewelry, Jo? You've got enough on tonight."

"Hey, Jo!" Patrice welcomes me with a big smile.

I didn't expect her to be so friendly. "I don't mean to bother you," I say, my fingers tightly gripping Sammi's phone. "I need to ask you something, then I'll go—"

"Don't be silly. You're not bothering us. Come and hang. Tanith, shove over and make room for Jo."

"That's okay," I say, taking a step back.

Patrice scoots to the edge of the table. She crooks her finger at me. I inch forward. Patrice puts a hand on my shoulder. "Sit. Down."

"Okay." I'm not sure it's a good idea to sit next to her.

"BTW, great outfit," she says, moving her black sweater to clear space beside her on the table. "Love the pearls, Quirky Chic, but don't they get in your way when you're dancing?"

"Uh . . . no. I haven't been dancing that much."

"Oh, that's too bad. I'm glad you came over. I've been wanting to talk to you. I wanted to say I was sorry for—you know, everything. I've decided I want us to be friends again."

"You are? You do?" I stare at her. This is a complete switch. I should be happy, right? This is what I wanted, right?

Patrice leans back against the wall. "So what did you want to ask?"

I hold Sammi's phone, tilting the screen toward Patrice. "I was . . . well, I was wondering, why is your photo on my sister's phone?"

"What are you talking about? What have you got there?" Tanith tries to lean over me. "What is that?"

I give her a sharp elbow to the ribs. "You really should stop asking so many questions, Tanith," I say, never taking my eyes off Patrice. "It's soooo annoying."

India snickers. She puts a hand up to muffle her laugh.

Patrice looks at the photo for a long time. She taps one of her front teeth thoughtfully, then finally glances at me and says, "I don't know."

I can feel my cheeks getting warm. "That's your answer? You don't know."

"It doesn't really seem fair to attack someone who isn't here to defend herself."

"Defend herself?" My pulse quickens. "Who are you talking about?"

"Isn't it obvious?" Patrice throws out a hand, nearly knocking the phone from my grip. "You sister is sure good at stealing things, Jo. First Noah, and then *my* photo!"

SEVENTEEN

Last Dance

"WANNA DANCE?"

"Okay," I croak.

I do my best to keep my trembling fingers steady as I put my hand in Noah's. I try to look happy, but inside I'm crumbling. It's a slow dance, but I can hardly hear the music. My heart is banging so hard against my chest I am sure it's going to break a couple of ribs. Patrice's words keep bombarding my brain.

Stay away from Noah. Stay away from Noah.

I couldn't believe what Patrice was asking— demanding. I stood in the girls' bathroom facing her for what seemed like hours, unable to speak. I kept waiting for her to say it was all a joke, but she didn't. Her satisfied expression told me she had carefully thought through every detail. She knew, and I knew, I was in a corner. Say no to Patrice and watch my sister live out her middle school days on the outer edge of the universe and hate me for it. Say yes and reunite Jorgianna with the only friend she'd ever had and desperately missed, even if that friend happens to be a slimy snake.

"Well?"

"Okay, Patrice. You win. I'll do it," I said. I didn't want to stay to see her gloat, so I bolted from the bathroom and ran smack into Eden on the other side of the door. I knocked her flat.

She's okay. Mrs. Vanderslice and I got her some ice for her bruised elbow, and she's resting near the snack bar. Eden wanted to know what happened with Patrice, of course. I said Patrice asked me for a small favor. It is the last lie I will ever tell my best friend. Soon I will explain everything. I will tell her the truth about Patrice and my photograph and the deal I made with her, but not tonight. Tonight I have to say good-bye to Noah. It is not helping that Bob Dylan is singing "Make You Feel My Love."

Noah puts his arms around me. I rest my head on his shoulder. It is our first dance. And our last. Once the song is over, I will have to start ignoring him. I close my eyes, my mind absorbing everything—the rhythm of his breathing, the slow *swish* of his feet, the warmth of his hands on my waist, the way his knee sometimes bumps mine. I need to remember every single thing that happens in the next two minutes so I can knit together a memory that will last for the rest of my life.

"Sammi?"

"Yes."

"Something wrong?"

My eyes fly open. He can sense something is upsetting me.

Not yet, Noah. One more minute. Please let me have one more verse.

I lift my head. The longer I wait, the harder this is going to be.

Do it. Do it now.

What do I say to him? That I don't melt when he says my name or walks me to class or shares his french fries in the park. What lie am I supposed to come up with to hurt the nicest boy in the world?

I pull back to look at him, my eyes filling with water. "Noah, I'm sorry but I have to . . . I need to . . ."

Looking past Noah's head, I see Jorgianna. She is shoulder to shoulder with Patrice on the table in the corner. They are huddled over her phone. Seeing them together chills me to the core.

What am I doing?

I can take my sister's anger and I can take the silent treatment, but I couldn't take it if she turned into a lying, cheating reptile like Patrice Houston. Jorgianna may never forgive me for damaging her friendship with Patrice, but I could never forgive myself for repairing it.

No. I won't do it. This ends now. Patrice has taken too much from me already. I will not let her take one thing more.

I look straight into those nice, nice green eyes. "I need . . . to go save my sister."

EIGHTEEN

The Genius Learns a Thing or Two

"I'M SUCH AN IDIOT." IN ONE MOTION, I JUMP OFF the table.

How could I be so blind?

"Jo, don't be hard on Sammi," says Patrice. "She's jealous of our friendship—"

"You are really something, Patrice."

"Thanks," she says, missing my sarcasm.

"For someone who is usually right about everything, I don't know how I could have been so wrong about you."

She starts to speak, but I don't give her the chance.

"When I met you," I say, "I thought you were so

strong and independent. You weren't afraid to tell the world 'This is who I am.' I admired you for that. But I was so busy looking *at* you, Patrice, I never stopped to look *behind* you." I take a good, hard look at Cara, Mercy, Desiree, India, and even Tanith—obnoxious, irritating Tanith. "If I had, I would have seen all the people you trample on every day. You're not a friend, you're a bully."

Patrice glares at me. Her icy stares will not work on me. Not anymore.

"I don't know how you got Sammi's photo," I say, "but I'll bet she does."

Tipping her head back against the wall, Patrice waves me away as if I am a mere peasant.

"I'll bet Mrs. Vanderslice would love to know too."

Patrice jerks up. "Wait a minute, Jo. Can't we talk about this?"

"And another thing." My whole body feels like it's on fire. "My name is not Jo. It's not Jo Jo or Jorgi either. My name is Jorgianna."

"Jorgianna!"

Is there an echo in here?

My sister is flying toward me. Sammi is weaving her way through kids like a basketball player on a fast break. Noah is one step behind her. Eden is hurrying behind him, a hand clamped to her temple to keep the silk flower in her hair.

"Patrice, no!" Sammi puts on the brakes, and I throw out an arm to catch her before she crashes into the table. "I won't do it. The deal is off. It's *off*."

"What deal?" I ask.

"Yes, what deal?" asks Patrice sweetly, easily stretching out her legs.

"I . . . I . . ." My sister's freckles are glowing. Frightened blue eyes probe mine. "Patrice said she would take you back as a friend if I . . . if I . . . didn't tell anyone that she stole my photo : . . and I had to promise to stay away from Noah."

Everyone gasps.

"Puh-lease," says Patrice. "That's a lie."

"No, it isn't," says another voice. India slides off the table and turns to face us. "Sammi is telling the truth. I was in the bathroom tonight. I overheard everything."

Patrice snorts. "No one believes *you*, India."

"I do." I plant my feet firmly next to India's brown sandals. "I believe her."

India smiles at me. "*Ačiū.*"

I look into my sister's glistening eyes. "You were really going to do that? You were going to give up your blue ribbon and Noah for me?"

A single nod sends a tear down her cheek.

I hold my sister's phone out to her. "You forgot something in the car."

She looks down, sees her photograph of the little girl at the aquarium, and the waterworks really begin. I put my arms around her and let her cry into my shoulder. Sammi has to bend way down and I have to go up on tiptoe, but she does and I do, and neither of us thinks a thing about it, because sisters do whatever they have to do to hold on to one another.

Sammi taught me that.

NINETEEN

A New World

"GIRLS, LET'S GET GOING! THE TRAFFIC REPORTER just gave the commute into the city an eight on the jam-factor scale."

"Coming, Mom," calls Jorgianna.

Down on one knee, I glance up at my sister. "Shouldn't we have some kind of ceremony or something?"

My sister and the four white angel clips in her hair flutter in agreement. "Short and sweet."

I hold up all the copies of our contract. "We promise never to have anything in writing between us ever again. Farewell, middle school contract. Good-bye and good riddance. Hit it, Jorgianna."

My sister presses the start button and I feed both copies of our contract into the shredder. I feel a sense of relief, watching the big metal teeth slice the pages into confetti. When the machine stops whirring, I stand up and dust off the knees of my black yoga pants.

Jorgianna unplugs the shredder, we grab our backpacks, then head out to the car. Mom backs out of the garage, and, for the first time since Jorgianna started middle school with me, I relax—really and truly relax. On the way to school Jorgianna and I look out our own windows, as we have always done, and still get lost in our own thoughts of the day ahead, as we have always done, but that mysterious force that once pushed us apart . . . is gone.

Jorgianna scoots toward me as far as her seatbelt will allow. "It would never have worked, you know."

"What?"

"Ignoring Noah."

"You don't think so?"

"Nope. You can't make somebody *not* like you, especially someone who likes you as much as he does."

I smile.

Mom pulls up to the drop-off curb next to the school. Jorgianna and I open our car doors together. We get out, say good-bye to Mom, and head into the building side by side. As we split apart to go to our own lockers, I say, "See you at lunch."

"Sammi, you don't have to—"

"It's all set. You're eating with Eden and me. Third table next to the windows. See you at noon."

She gives me a grin, but doesn't argue. Jorgianna bounces away in my once-beloved hunter-green Daisy Chain boots. Four sets of lacy angel's wings wave to me. I wave back. I watch until her emerald-green jumper and red tights turn the corner. Sheesh. All that's missing are the reindeer.

I head for first period.

Ding-dee-ding. Ding-dee-ding. Ding. Ding. Ding. Dong.

Today's instrument is a row of juice glasses, each filled with a different amount of water. Miss

Fleischmann is rapping on them with a couple of small metal curtain rods. She is so into her performance she doesn't greet me. I melt into my seat. Eden and Charlie both have the same "get me out of here" look I am sure is on my own face.

After taking attendance, Miss Fleischmann says, "We'll be going to the library so you can research your poet biographies today. Before we go, I have your fairy tales to hand back."

My stomach slides into my toes.

This is it.

I let my head fall back. Close my eyes. Listen for the gentle smack of paper against my desk, and when it comes I take a long, deep, terrified breath.

Please, please, please, let it be an A. Not another blah B. Just one little, itty-bitty, teen-weeny, pointy-hatted A.

I open my eyes. Hold the air in my lungs. Flip the pages over . . .

An A-plus!

Hallelujah! My first A in Miss Fleischmann's class, and it only took eight months. It's gorgeous—a sweeping teepee shape in red marker with a little curly cue at the end of each leg. I trace my finger over it. A for

Amazing! Plus, a plus! Miss Fleischmann has written her comments below the grade.

This is a touching and emotional story, Sammi! Seraphina's pain at having to leave her family was heart wrenching. I knew you could do it! Great work!

I cannot wait to show this to Jorgianna.

The second I enter the cafeteria, I begin looking for my sister. I also start to get worried. Patrice may not have my sister under her thumb anymore, but she is still the most popular girl in school. Saturn has a lot of influence in our universe. What if Patrice starts spreading gossip about Jorgianna? What if Jorgianna doesn't make any new friends? What if—?

Stop it. Stop 'what if-ing.'

"Do you see her?" I ask Eden, my voice shaky. We are standing by our table so Jorgianna can easily spot us.

"No, not yet."

"Where could she be? I told her where to meet us."

"It's only two minutes after. She'll be here."

"You can't miss her. She looks like one of Santa's elves. She's got on a green jumper, red tights, and a bunch of angel clips in her hair. Maybe I should go look for her—"

"There she is." Eden spins me toward the south entrance.

We wave like mad until Jorgianna sees us. She is not alone.

"Can I bring a friend or two?" asks my sister as she approaches.

"Sure." I grin at India, who is right behind her. "There's plenty of room."

"Good," says Jorgianna. She throws an arm into the air. "Hanna! Lauren! Over here."

The pair is getting their lunches at the deli counter. Hanna puts up a hand. "Be right there."

Eden tugs at my sleeve. "We should have done that a long time ago, you know."

I know.

"Where do we sit?" asks India.

"Anywhere you want," I say.

"What do we eat?"

"Anything you want," says Jorgianna. "I'm getting a taco and some peanut butter cookies." She bends in close to India, and I hear her say, "And I can promise nobody here will ask you for money."

"Really?" India's face lights up. "It's like a whole new world."

"It sure is," I say, then quietly to Eden, "and as far from Saturn as possible."

Pinky lock.

"Skuh-wee!"

TWENTY

Going Up

THREE WEEKS LATER . . .

My knees are wobbly, my palms damp. I stay still, daring only to let my eyes wander beyond the railing as the metal steps take me farther from the ground. I don't understand why we couldn't have taken the regular stairs. Cement stairs don't grab your sleeves or skirt. They don't suck you in. I am only on this escalator because Sammi is with me. She is one step below me, directly behind my right shoulder. Banana, Mom, and Dad are several steps behind us.

"I can't believe I let you dye my hair," says Sammi.

Carefully, I turn to look at her. Thanks to the step, we are almost at eye level. "You look cute."

She twirls a lock of hair around her index finger. "I feel like everybody is staring at me."

"You can barely see it. Maybe next time you'll let me do more than one strand in a color that *isn't* already on your head."

"We'll see."

This has to be the longest escalator on earth. We continue climbing and climbing, gliding toward the glass ceiling of the state convention center. I rub my palms against the hips of my lime-green sparkly dress that Banana gave me—another great score from her thrift store. I check again to be sure that my left gossamer wing of a sleeve isn't too close to the rubber handrail. If I had known I was going to have to ride the Stairs of Death, I would never have worn a dress with such wide sleeves. I never know when to get off these things. Too early and you trip. Too late and you trip. Either way, it's a disaster waiting to happen.

"Nervous?" asks Sammi.

"Yes."

Smoothing the front of her pink sleeveless dress, she gives me a sideways grin. "Don't be."

"Why not?" I study her. She is too calm. "You know something. What do you know?"

My sister untangles one of my dragonfly earrings. "Mrs. Vanderslice called last night."

"And?"

"I'm not supposed to tell."

"Sammi!"

Topaz blue eyes crinkle. "But nobody told me I couldn't say how much Banana and I are looking forward to seeing our nation's capital."

"The capital?"

The capital is Washington, D.C. And Washington, D.C. is where they are holding the national student art show. Oh my gosh!

"Close your mouth," she whispers. "Turn around. One other thing, Jorgianna."

"What?"

"I'm proud of you. Always was. Always will be."

"Same here," I say. I let myself relax, because I know I can stop counting now. I can stop counting how many times I win, because for the rest of our lives this is how it is going to be. When I win, Sammi wins, and vice-versa.

"Hey, girls!" calls Dad.

I glance over my right shoulder. Sammi looks over her left.

"Complementary colors," he says. His eyes move from Sammi's pink dress, also a gift from Banana, to my green one. "You know what that means, don't you?"

We glance at one another. We know. We bring out the best in each other.

We are almost to the top of the escalator. I hope I can do this without tripping. Or getting sucked in. Or dying. As the mechanical steps slide over the curve of the summit, there is a hand on my elbow. "I'm here," Sammi's calm voice fills my ear. "Ready?"

"Ready," I whisper back.

"Step now."

* Acknowledgments *

Special thanks to:

Rosemary Stimola, my insightful and delightful agent; Alyson Heller, editor/cheerleader extraordinaire; Mom and Dad, the best parents a girl could have; and, as ever, William, whose love makes all things possible.

Check out these great titles from Aladdin M!X:

ALADDINMIX.COM